CHAMBRUN PRESSED THE "REPLAY" BUTTON ON THE ~~~~~.

The tape made a whirring soun~~~~~ we heard a male voice.

"Pierre Chambrun?"

"Speaking." That was Chambrun.

"You've been treading on pretty thin ice over there, Chambrun. I warned you." A slightly British or Irish voice, as Chambrun had guessed.

Chambrun again: "One of your people murdered one of my people. There was no way I could block off the police."

"I know. Wrong man meets wrong man at the wrong moment. But you've got to get things back to normal during the next twenty-four hours—or else."

"How is Miss Ruysdale?"

"I suppose I could say 'fine.' Fine but not happy."

"Put Miss Ruysdale on."

"Why not?"

There was a moment's silence and then Betsy Ruysdale spoke. There was no questioning her voice.

"Pierre? Pierre, listen to me. You have to forget about me and do what you have to do."

There was the sound of an angry male voice in the background and Betsy Ruysdale was gone.

———————— ★ ————————

"Well-written, well-paced and laced with intriguing people."

—*Morning Advocate* (Baton Rouge)

HUGH PENTECOST

MURDER IN HIGH PLACES

WORLDWIDE.

TORONTO • NEW YORK • LONDON
AMSTERDAM • PARIS • SYDNEY • HAMBURG
STOCKHOLM • ATHENS • TOKYO • MILAN
MADRID • WARSAW • BUDAPEST • AUCKLAND

MURDER IN HIGH PLACES

A Worldwide Mystery/April 1992

First published by Dodd, Mead & Company Inc.

ISBN 0-373-26094-6

Part One

ONE

THERE ARE certain things in our daily lives that we take for granted, like the rising of the sun. It is a miraculous event to which we pay almost no attention. It will happen and we have no anxiety that it will not happen. We don't believe that even God Himself will interfere with that certainty. But what if one day it did not rise, if there was no daylight?

Something as unbelievable as that happened in my world, which is the Beaumont, New York City's top luxury hotel. I am Mark Haskell, the hotel's public relations man for the last eleven years. Every day as I move through various departments and areas of the hotel I see dozens of things going on that are so familiar that I don't really notice them. They are supposed to happen and they do happen because of the Swiss-watch efficiency of the organization designed by the Man. "The Man" is Pierre Chambrun, the Beaumont's legendary manager. In the world of the Beaumont, Chambrun is king, the mayor of a city within a city. You might even say Chambrun is God in the world of the Beaumont.

But even God has to have subordinates he can count on completely. I suppose the single most important person to Chambrun in the daily running of his hotel is his incomparable secretary, Betsy Ruysdale. Chambrun neuters this handsome, copper-haired woman in her late thirties by calling her "Ruysdale," never "Betsy" or "Miss Ruysdale," but rumor persists that in secret times and secret places the lady is much more to her boss than simply an efficiency expert.

Every day of my life begins the same way. I am up the night before till three or four in the morning, till all the bars, and the Blue Lagoon nightclub have closed and the customers have retired to their rooms or, if they are casuals, have gone home. I sleep for four and a half hours, am called by the operator on the hotel switchboard, shower, shave, and dress, and go down the hall to Chambrun's second-floor office.

At precisely nine o'clock the special chef is removing Chambrun's gourmet breakfast from his office, which is more like a magnificent living room than a place of business—paintings, including a Picasso given to Chambrun by the painter himself, Oriental rugs, Florentine and French carved furniture. Betsy Ruysdale will be standing by his desk as I enter, a stack of registration cards brought for Chambrun's perusal. These cards will tell him who has checked in since yesterday morning. The reason for my presence each day for this view of the registration cards was that if we had a new guest of importance, a foreign diplomat, a Hollywood movie star, a famous figure in the arts, someone who wanted special attention—anonymity or a big press ballyhoo—it would be my job to handle the press.

I suppose I could call it "the morning the sun didn't come up." It was a beautiful August day, not a cloud in the sky, a cool breeze drifting from the city's canyons from the northeast. I walked through Betsy Ruysdale's deserted office and into the inner sanctum at precisely nine o'clock. Things were not as they always were. Chambrun was standing behind his carved Florentine desk, drumming impatiently on its edge with his squarish fingers. He is a short, stocky, dark man with heavy pouches under dark eyes that twinkle with humor or, if he's displeased, turn cold as a hanging judge's. I have written many accounts of adventures at the Beaumont, and a movie company, considering film possibilities, had asked me to suggest an actor who could play the role of Pierre Chambrun. Unfortunately, the actor who would have been perfect is no longer with us, the late Claude Rains, jaunty, elegant, witty, but with an interior of cold, hard steel. Chambrun was the hanging judge at this moment and I knew why. I knew the reason at once. Betsy Ruysdale wasn't there, nor were the registration cards.

Chambrun glanced at his wristwatch. "Ruysdale must have overslept," he said. "Would you be good enough to call her apartment, Mark? Her number's on my emergency phone list."

Betsy Ruysdale never overslept. She was never not exactly where Chambrun needed her to be, morning, noon, or night. I dialed her apartment, which is less than a block from the hotel. No answer. I called the front desk and talked to Paul Atterbury, the head clerk. I asked him if Miss Ruysdale had picked up the reservation cards.

"Not yet," Atterbury told me. "I was beginning to wonder."

"Have someone else bring them up," I said, and turned back to Chambrun. "You're sure she didn't tell you she was going to be late this morning?"

He didn't answer. It was obvious he wouldn't be fretting if he'd known in advance that she wouldn't be here on time. The little red light was blinking on the phone on his desk. Betsy should have been there to answer it.

"Tell the switchboard to hold all calls until we can get a girl up here from the stenographic pool to screen calls for us," Chambrun said.

I gave his message to Ora Veach, the chief telephone operator, asked her to get us a girl from the steno pool, and also asked her if she'd heard anything from Betsy Ruysdale. She hadn't.

"Call the local police precinct," Chambrun said. "There may have been an accident."

"Hadn't I better get Jerry Dodd to go over to her apartment?" I asked. Jerry is the hotel's security chief.

"She may be sick, or fainted, or had a fall or something."

"Thanks for thinking, Mark," Chambrun said. "And then call the police."

I could take a lot more space than it merits to go into all of the moves that were made to locate the missing Betsy Ruysdale. Jerry Dodd, a wiry little man, tough as nails, a former FBI agent, had gone to Betsy's apartment. It was an old brownstone, with no doorman, night or day. Jerry located the janitor, who let him into Betsy's apartment. She wasn't there.

"No doorman," Jerry told Chambrun, "so there's no one who saw her arrive home last night or leave this morning. Place is neat as a pin, bed made up. No way to tell whether she slept in it last night, made it up this morning, or whether she never got home at all last night."

The police reported no accident in the neighborhood during the night or this morning. No employee on the night shift at the hotel or this morning's shift had seen Betsy.

The impossible had happened. Betsy Ruysdale, as reliable and dependable as the rising sun, had disappeared into thin air.

I REMEMBER talking to a psychiatrist friend of mine one time—not professionally. I was telling him about my feelings at being kept waiting for an hour by a chick who'd agreed to let me buy her dinner.

"I found myself afraid that she'd been in some kind of accident, hit by a taxi or a truck, instead of guessing at the much more likely thing—that her hairdresser had made her late."

My shrink friend gave me a cynical smile. "You don't read yourself correctly, Mark," he told me. "You weren't *afraid* she'd been hit by a truck, you *hoped* she'd been hit by a truck. Anything less would be a threat to your image of yourself as an irresistible male!"

I wondered about Chambrun that morning—"the morning the sun didn't rise" at the Beaumont. Was he calling the cops, the hospitals, sounding alarms and excursions, because he felt that anything less than a disaster would reduce his image of himself as a boss whose trusted employee would never let him down? There would be, I told myself, a simple and probably comic explanation for Betsy Ruysdale's tardiness on that August morning.

But things didn't run with their usual smoothness that first hour of no Ruysdale. Chambrun didn't seem able to concentrate on the registration cards. Each time the little red light winked on the phone I could see him grow tense, waiting for Dolly Malone, the girl from the steno pool who was now installed at Ruysdale's desk, to put the call through to him. Chambrun had instructed Dolly not to put through any casual calls, and in that first hour none came through. Chambrun was chain-smoking his flat Egyptian cigarettes. I think it came to him as a shock when he went over to the Turkish coffee maker on the sideboard and found there was no coffee. Ruysdale had been preparing that hair-raising brew for him every morning for years. Not today.

At precisely ten o'clock Dolly Malone put through a call. Chambrun had the intercom system turned on, so I could hear the conversation.

"Mr. Welch is here, Mr. Chambrun," Dolly said.

"Who the hell is Mr. Welch?" Chambrun asked.

"I don't know, sir, but Miss Ruysdale has him down on your appointment pad for ten o'clock."

"I don't know a Mr. Welch!"

"Under his name on the appointment pad is another name," Dolly told the Man. "Claude Perrault."

"Damn!" Chambrun said. I'd never seen him as scattered as he seemed to be that morning. "Hold Mr. Welch for five minutes and then send him in," he told Dolly. He hung up the phone and looked at me. "You ever hear of someone named Lawrence Welch?" he asked me.

It didn't ring a bell with me.

He shuffled papers on his desk, almost aimlessly. "Ruysdale would have had a file on him for me," he said. "Lawrence Welch—Larry Welch."

"Larry Welch is something else again," I said, my personal computer starting to work. "He's a political journalist and writer, half a dozen books. Rates up along with people like Teddy White—*Making of the President* stuff. Claude Perrault doesn't mean anything to me.''

''Friend of mine from the old days,'' Chambrun said, ''the Black Days.''

Way back around 1940 a French boy in his late teens named Pierre Chambrun had come to America to study hotel management at Cornell. A year and a half later he was on his way back to join the French army, which was in total rout at the hands of the Nazis by the time he got there. Chambrun joined the French Resistance, fighting the brutal occupation of Paris by the Germans. He rarely talked about that time in his life, but when he did he referred to it as ''the Black Days.''

Chambrun picked up his phone. ''I'm ready for Mr. Welch,'' he told Dolly.

The man who came into the inner sanctum was almost a startling double for Burt Reynolds, the movie actor, dark hair, a dark mustache, a bright, white-toothed smile, laughing blue eyes. He crossed straight to the Man, holding out his hand—ignoring me, by the way.

''This is a long-looked-forward-to pleasure, Mr. Chambrun,'' he said. ''Once he gets started, Claude can never stop talking about you.''

''That was another time, another world,'' Chambrun said. He wasn't clicking on all cylinders. He should know why Welch was here, and he clearly didn't. The facts he should have were somewhere with Betsy Ruysdale.

"I haven't registered," Welch said, "because I thought I should check in with you first. I mean, if the penthouse isn't ready for me? . . ."

That seemed to make sense to Chambrun. "Ah, yes, the guest penthouse," he said. He introduced me to Welch and asked me to call the front desk and check with Atterbury. "Find out if Penthouse Three is ready for Mr. Smith."

"Who is Mr. Smith?" I asked.

Welch grinned at me. "I guess I am," he said.

Atterbury told me all was in order for "Mr. Smith," and I nodded to Chambrun.

"Tell Atterbury I'll arrange to register him later," Chambrun said. He turned to Welch. "Your luggage?"

"A suitcase in your outer office and this," Welch said, patting a bulky briefcase he had tucked under his left arm. "I hope Haskell won't mind if we have a short talk alone, Mr. Chambrun."

"Mark is one of my closest people," Chambrun said. I felt myself grow a couple of inches. "If you need help, or assistance of any kind, he'll be your man. I'd like him to stay."

That didn't seem to please Welch. His bright smile had faded.

"I'd trust Mark with my life," Chambrun said. "I trust him with yours."

Welch decided, with some reluctance, I thought, to go along. "Claude assured me the security in the penthouse was rather special," he said.

"It is rather special as far as privacy is concerned," Chambrun said. "It's not a fortress, Mr. Welch. I'm not sure I'd want it used as a fortress."

"Will you tell me what the setup is there?" Welch asked.

"There are forty-four floors to the hotel," Chambrun said. "The roof is the forty-fifth. There are three penthouses."

"Three?" Welch sounded surprised.

"I live in one," Chambrun said. "A very elegant octogenarian lady lives in the second one. The third is reserved for special guests like yourself—usually foreign diplomats here for United Nations business."

"If there are three separate living apartments up on the roof, that means there must be considerable traffic up there—back and forth." Welch was frowning. "Claude Perrault gave me to understand that—"

"I don't know what Claude gave you to understand, Mr. Welch. And so far I don't quite understand your concern. You want privacy, I can guarantee it. Only one of the elevators in the hotel goes all the way to the roof. I use it, Mrs. Haven, the lady in Penthouse Two, uses it, and whoever may be occupying Penthouse Three uses it. The operator who handles that particular elevator takes no one to the roof without first clearing it with me, or Mrs. Haven, or whoever is occupying Penthouse Three. The roof area is not available to sightseers or rubberneckers, Mr. Welch."

Larry Welch still seemed to be hesitant about talking freely. I guessed it was me. Claude Perrault had guaranteed Chambrun but not, apparently, anyone else.

"I've just remembered something I must do," I said. "If you'll excuse me—" I started for the door.

"Mark!" Chambrun's voice was sharp. He was still on edge about Betsy Ruysdale. "Stay, please." He turned to Welch. "The operation of a hotel like this is a little more complex than you may imagine, Mr. Welch. Every detail of its functioning is very precise. If you have something confidential to tell me that relates in any way to running the hotel, you'd better know that I will share what you tell me with at least three other people: there will be Mark; my secretary, Miss Ruysdale; and my chief of security, Jerry Dodd. If you require anything special of me and I should be unavailable, then someone else must be able to carry on without having to delay for explanations from you. Mark, Miss Ruysdale, and Dodd are extensions of me. If you can trust me, you can trust them. If you can't trust me—well, I have a hotel to run, Mr. Welch."

Welch hesitated a second or two, and then his face lit up with his bright, disarming smile. "Trusting people is something I've spent my professional life learning not to do, Mr. Chambrun," he said. "Being a journalist, I find that people tend to tell me what they want me to believe rather than real facts. My instinct warns me not to tell anyone anything I don't want made public until I'm ready to make it public myself."

"You'll have to make your own decision, Mr. Welch," Chambrun said. He kept glancing at the far door as if he expected Betsy Ruysdale to suddenly materialize.

Welch let his breath out in a long sigh. "So—I'll tell you what you need to know," he said. He turned to me. "Holding back had nothing to do with you personally, Haskell. Just a lifelong habit." He put his attaché case down on the edge of Chambrun's desk. "In this briefcase, Chambrun, are the ingredients that just might start World War Three."

"Forgive me if I say that sounds a bit extravagant, Mr. Welch," Chambrun said.

"I know," Welch said. "God help me, I know. But let me tell you what I feel free to tell you. In this briefcase are letters, photographs, photostats of documents all relating to one man—who for the time being must remain nameless. This man holds a very important position, very high up in the government of our country. In the process of gathering material on the complex and volatile situation in the Middle East—Arabs versus Israel, Iran versus Iraq, Egypt and Israel, the involvement of powerful outside forces like the United States and Russia—I kept coming across this nameless man's trail. From thinking of him in the beginning as being a key figure working in the interests of the United States, I eventually began to wonder whose side he was really on. He appeared to be a double or triple agent, working for two or three sides at the same time."

"But really working primarily for himself?" Chambrun suggested.

Larry Welch nodded. "And getting fabulously rich by selling out first one side and then the other. Well, I found myself getting less and less interested in the story I'd set out to research and more and more fascinated by this one man. Fascinated, and scared half out of my wits, Mr. Chambrun, as I began to see the possibilities for a monumental explosion if someone doesn't stop this conniving sonofabitch before he goes too far."

Chambrun was drumming on the edge of his desk with his fingers, wondering about Ruysdale, I knew. "If what you suggested is so, Mr. Welch, you have the material in your briefcase to do just that—stop him."

Welch grinned. "To quote the Bard—'Aye, there's the rub.'" He reached in his pocket and produced a cigarette and a lighter. He drew smoke deep into his lungs and exhaled in an almost exhausted-sounding sigh. "To reveal what I have found out about my man will also expose the treachery of certain Arab leaders and terrorists, diplomats from countries we think of as friendly, heads of huge international corporations.

To put it bluntly, Mr. Chambrun, to reveal what I know about this man may set off the same disaster I'm afraid will happen if I do nothing. Dead if I do, and dead if I don't.''

"May I ask what this has to do with me, with my hotel, and with Penthouse Three?" Chambrun asked.

"It's a decision I can't make all by myself," Welch said. "To reveal or not to reveal. What's in that briefcase is dynamite. I need other people, men in high places, to look at it and help decide what's to be done. It's not as simple as it sounds. The man whose record is in that briefcase knows what I've been up to. Obviously, certain of his treacherous friends know. My life isn't worth a lead penny at the moment. It could happen to me on the street. I could be poisoned in a restaurant. They might even kill me while I sleep. Your friend Claude Perrault, a man I trust, suggested your hotel might be a sanctuary for me. He told me you could keep me safe here while the people I need to consult come here to look at the evidence I have. The whole process will take a few days. The men I must consult have seen my evidence, the decision will not be mine to make, and the personal danger to me will, at least, diminish. If you tell me to go peddle my papers somewhere else, Mr. Chambrun, and I walk out of your hotel now, that may be that.''

Chambrun hesitated a moment. He reached for his Turkish coffee, which, for the first time ever, wasn't there. "Right out of a spy novel," he said.

Welch smiled his bright smile. "Isn't it?" he said.

Chambrun, who never fidgets, was fidgeting. His mind was on Ruysdale, who was now more than two hours late. "Let me tell you how it is, Mr. Welch," he said. "I don't run a sanctuary against violence here at the Beaumont. I provide the best in service, in food, in wine, in entertainment. And I promise privacy for famous people who don't want to be bothered by reporters, cameras, autograph hounds, and just plain rubberneckers. I can provide you with all those things plus the rather special seclusion of Penthouse Three. But I cannot supply you with bodyguards, and I am loath to have would-be assassins stalking my corridors. I am obligated to all my guests, not just one with special problems. Under normal circumstances I would do just what you suggested—tell you to go peddle your papers somewhere else."

"But?" Welch asked, still smiling.

"A long, long time ago," Chambrun said, his eyes narrowed, "the Nazis had a price on my head in Paris. I would have died then, slowly and very unpleasantly, if it hadn't been for Claude Perrault. He has asked me to help and protect you, Mr. Welch, a friend of his. I owe him that much and more. So, Mark will install you in Penthouse Three, explain the routines to you, and I will instruct our security people to keep a special eye out for you. And now, if you will excuse me, I have a somewhat understaffed hotel to run."

"I'm more than grateful, Mr. Chambrun," Welch said.

"Thank Claude Perrault," Chambrun said.

I TOOK Larry Welch down the hallway and rang the special bell for the roof elevator. Welch wouldn't let his precious briefcase out of his hands, so I carried his bag, which seemed to weigh a ton. As we waited for the elevator, Welch remarked that he had somehow expected a warmer, more outgoing person in Chambrun than he had found.

"You turned up on a bad day," I told him. "His secretary, who is his right arm, hasn't turned up this morning, and without explanation or any word."

"Boyfriend?" Welch suggested.

"Maybe, but I think not," I said. "We've been checking police, hospitals, the works. Nothing."

The elevator door opened and we were confronted by Dick Berger, the day operator. Dick, a blond boy of German extraction, has a rather stiff, professional smile. He is more than just an elevator operator. He is enrolled in Jerry Dodd's security force and gets paid a salary that would have made the other operators green with envy if they'd known.

"This is Mr. Lawrence Welch," I told Dick. "He's going to be in Penthouse Three for a few days."

"Good morning, sir," Dick said.

"Mr. Welch is to get Treatment A," I told Dick.

We got into the car and started the noiseless climb to the roof. "Has Mark explained to you how Treatment A works, Mr. Welch?" Dick asked.

"Sounds like a massage under a sunlamp," Welch said, laughing.

"See this little phone here in the car?" Dick asked, pointing to the instrument. The phone has three buttons on it, one, two, and three. It connects with the three penthouses on the roof. Dick went on to explain. "There is an instrument just like this next to your regular phone in Penthouse Three. It connects only with this phone in the car. If someone asks to be taken up to the roof to see you, Mr. Welch, I call you on this phone. I give you the name your caller has given me. If you say yes I bring him up. If you say no, I turn him away."

"Anybody can give you any name," Welch said, his smile gone.

"You will describe the person for me if you have any doubts. If you want, I will ask him for an ID. I don't bring him till you say yes."

"You aren't on this car twenty-four hours a day," Welch said.

"There are three of us in eight-hour shifts," Dick said, "Lucky Lewis, Bob Ballard, and me. Always someone who will handle visitors just the same way."

"Someone who asks for Mr. Chambrun, or the lady in Penthouse Two—"

"Mrs. Haven," Dick said.

"Someone who asks for them would have access to Penthouse Three once they got up to the roof, wouldn't they?"

"Yes, but neither one of them receives strangers they don't know," Dick said.

"Fire stairs?" Welch asked. "Couldn't someone take one of the other elevators to the forty-fourth floor and then come up the fire stairs?"

"The fire stairs lock on the inside," I told Welch. "Let people out, not in. It's about as foolproof as you can make it, Mr. Welch, unless you don't trust Chambrun or Mrs. Haven."

"I guess I have to, don't I?" Welch said.

The view of New York and its mammoth skyscrapers and its guarding rivers from the roof of the Beaumont is pretty spectacular on a day like this. Welch and I had only taken a few steps toward Penthouse 3 at the far end of the roof when we were greeted by a small but hostile sound.

"I forgot to mention another source of protection," I said. "We call him Mrs. Haven's Japanese gentleman friend."

At that moment from around the corner of Penthouse 2 came a small, black and white Japanese spaniel, snubnosed and about as unfriendly as a gargoyle.

The lady was right behind him, wearing a wide-brimmed straw hat and gardening gloves. Victoria Haven grows flowers of every conceivable variety in the fenced-in space behind her penthouse. If I told you I have a kind of crush on Victoria Haven, you might be inclined to laugh. She admits, without hesitation, that she was born in the year 1900, and Chambrun suggests she may be cheating a little. She is tall, stands very straight, and has a mass of henna-colored hair, a color that God never intended for humans. Her face is wrinkled, but her high cheekbones, wide, generous mouth, and bright blue eyes are remnants of very great beauty. Many years ago when parts of the Beaumont were co-op apartments she had bought Penthouse 2 and lived there ever since. "With my Japanese friend," she would tell anyone who asked. The spaniel's name is Toto, and there must have been five or six of them over the years, identical in appearance and disposition. It indicated some kind of special drag Victoria Haven has with Chambrun, because pets are not allowed in the Beaumont. Toto not only lives on the roof with his mistress, but every afternoon at five o'clock he goes down to the Trapeze Bar with her, where he sits beside her on his own red satin cushion and looks with contempt at the people who crowd around his great lady for conversation and old-world charm—and very modern wit.

"Toto, do go somewhere and be silent!" Victoria said.

I introduced my companion to her. "Mr. Welch will be staying in Penthouse Three for a few days."

"You're Larry Welch, the writer, aren't you?" the lady said. "I read your book on the assassination of President Sadat with interest and, I must admit, confusion. What a tangled web!"

"I'm flattered if you found it good reading, Mrs. Haven," Welch said.

"If we're to be neighbors, you might as well call me Victoria. I should tell you I've never liked it shortened to Vicky. There's always a drink in my place, Larry, if you get lonely. Perhaps you can unlock the mysteries of the Middle East for me."

Welch gave her a quick, sharp look and then smiled again. "I just might be able to do that," he said. "You can depend on it. I'll come knocking, Victoria—if Toto doesn't take my arm off."

"Like most men," Victoria said, "Toto threatens a lot, but he isn't much for real action. Well, I must get back to my tulips."

She turned and left us, Toto giving us a snort and following behind.

Watching her, Larry Welch shook his head. "Did I understand Chambrun to say 'octogenarian'?"

"Most popular chorus girl on Broadway, just after World War One," I told him.

"She's still got a great pair of legs," Larry Welch said.

"And wants you to notice them," I said. We'd reached the front door of Penthouse 3. I'd brought keys from Chambrun's office and I opened up what was to be Welch's hide-out for the next few days.

"This the only way in—this front door?" he asked.

"There's a back door. You've got an awninged terrace out there, view of the East River. Running hot or cold martinis can be arranged."

Larry's light mood had gone. "Locks like this?" He was pointing at the double snap locks and the chain on the inside of the front door.

"Back door like this, too," I said. "It makes some of our guests feel secure. They can be left unlocked and you'll be just as safe."

"Maid service? Room service?" he asked.

"When you want the maid to do her thing, ask for her. You want meals or drinks served, all you have to do is pick up the phone."

"Anyone can pose as a maid or a waiter," he said.

"We've had some pretty nervous people who were just as hot or hotter than you staying here," I said. "Nothing's ever happened to any of them."

"There's always a first time," Larry said, frowning.

I didn't take that as a prophecy, not then.

WHEN I'D GIVEN Larry the guided tour of the three-bedroom penthouse with its three baths, kitchen, and well-stocked liquor cabinet—drinks were on the house if you stay in this place—and showed him his two phones, the one to the outside world and the one to the private elevator, I left him. If Ruysdale hadn't been heard from, Chambrun was going to be sky-high. He would have discovered in the first three hours of this working day how many things Ruysdale did to keep things running smoothly without his really knowing she was doing them.

Dolly Malone was still at Ruysdale's desk when I got back to the second floor.

"The Man is on the move somewhere," she told me, "checking on everyone who might possibly have seen Betsy somewhere. I suggested family, somebody suddenly sick, but Mr. Chambrun says she doesn't have any family."

"He is her family," I said.

"He's asked for a dozen things I've never heard of," Dolly said. "You wouldn't believe the things she must do for him, have ready for him before he asks. I think you have to be some kind of genius to work for him."

"You have to know him," I said. "Betsy's had years to learn."

"You know something, Mark? If she doesn't show up soon, he may have to close down the hotel!" She was only half kidding.

I started circulating down on the lobby level, looking for Chambrun. It was getting on toward noon, and the early lunch crowd was beginning to sift into the hotel. Those so-called three-martini lunches begin in the Trapeze Bar on the mezzanine, the Spartan Bar, the Grill Room, and the main dining room at the lobby level. I sensed a kind of tension among the staff. Johnny Thacker, the day bell captain, said it best for all of them.

"Betsy would never not show without letting the Man know. Something bad has to have happened to her."

There were things I should be doing, but I wasn't. There was a luncheon for Republican Women Voters in one of the private dining rooms. I should have been checking to see if everything was in order. I left that to chance. I had to find Chambrun. If he needed help, I wanted to be there to help him.

I got on his trail a few minutes later through Waters, the doorman on the Fifth Avenue side of the hotel. Waters is a big, pleasant, gray-haired guy who has worn the Beaumont's doorman's uniform forever.

"He went out of the hotel, Mr. Haskell, about forty minutes ago," Waters told me. "Not like himself."

"How do you mean?"

"You know how he is. Always stops to say hello, asks me about my family, my kids, my grandchild. Even remembers their names. This time he just walked by me. I asked him if he wanted me to get him a taxi. He didn't answer, just walked on north up the avenue."

Leaving the hotel in the middle of the day was a rarity for Chambrun. That was the time when guests, members of the hotel's board of directors, and just friends would be looking for him. With Ruysdale missing, I couldn't imagine him leaving, in case there might be some word from her or about her.

From the front desk I called Dolly Malone up in Ruysdale's office. "Did he say where he was going, Dolly?"

"No. He just walked out."

"Was there any phone call?"

"The police called him just before he walked out," she said.

"Did you listen in on the call?"

"He didn't tell me to."

Ruysdale would have known, without being told, that kind of call should be monitored, probably recorded, at least notes taken. I called the police precinct and talked to the captain there. As far as he knew, no one had called Chambrun.

"Unfortunately, we have nothing to call about," he told me. "Not a sniff of the missing lady. We've got a general alarm out on her. Some cop out on the beat might have called Chambrun, but if it was anything important, he'd also have checked in here."

About an hour later, twenty past one to be exact, I was at the front desk talking to Atterbury when I saw Chambrun come in the Fifth Avenue entrance. He looked straight at me—or anyway through me, because he didn't speak—and headed toward the elevators. Several people tried to speak to him, but he was like a runner in a marathon, concentrating on the last few yards to the winning tape. He just kept going, stepped into the roof car with Dick Berger, and was gone.

Fifteen minutes later somebody flagged me down to tell me that Chambrun wanted to see me in his penthouse. Jerry Dodd reached the roof car at the same time I did. He'd also been summoned.

"He's heard something about Ruysdale, or he has some plan of action," Jerry suggested.

Dick Berger didn't have to go through any of his telephone routines with us. Jerry and Ruysdale and I didn't have to get permission from anyone to go up to the penthouse level. You could say we had season passes.

I rang the doorbell of Penthouse 1 when we got there, and there was a clicking sound, which meant that Chambrun was pressing the trip-lock button by his desk in the living room. Jerry and I went in and then down the short foyer to the living room.

Chambrun was standing with his back to us by the French windows that looked out onto his terrace. In the distance I could see Victoria Haven working among her brightly colored tulips. Chambrun didn't turn to greet us.

"Thank you both for coming," he said. It was a voice I'd never heard before, flat, cold, colorless. Jerry and I glanced at each other. "I wanted to tell you that I've heard from Ruysdale."

"Oh, great!" Jerry said. "Is she okay."

"She's fine," Chambrun said. He still didn't turn to look at us. "A personal emergency that will keep her away for a few days."

"Without letting you know in advance?" I asked.

"She'd asked someone else to get to me, but there was some kind of slip up. What I want you two to do is spread the word among the staff that the emergency is over. The lost is found."

"I don't mind telling you, boss, this will relieve a lot of us," Jerry said.

"So, get to it, please," Chambrun said, still not turning.

Jerry and I started for the door.

"Wait!" It was almost a shout from Chambrun.

He had turned and I almost didn't recognize him. His face was like a gray rock in which deep grooves had been etched. His mouth was a thin knife slit.

"I can't do it," he said.

"Do what, boss?" Jerry asked.

Chambrun sank down in the armchair near the windows. For a moment he lowered his head and covered his face with his hands. In all the years I've worked for him and with him I'd never seen a moment of weakness like this. I saw his shoulders heave, as if he'd actually been choking off a sob.

Then he lowered his hands, stood up, and faced us. "Ruysdale is not safe, is not involved in some personal business," he said. "She has been kidnapped."

It was too far out to make sense to me for a moment, but Jerry Dodd was right on the ball. "Ransom?" he asked.

"You might call it that. I am instructed to do certain things if I want to see Ruysdale alive again. If I do what they tell me to do, I will become an accessory to murder. If I don't do what they tell me to do, I will also become an accessory to murder, Ruysdale's murder!"

TWO

IT HAD BEGUN with that call Dolly Malone had mentioned from the "police."

"Voice I never heard before," Chambrun told us. "Not a typical American speech pattern. English, Irish, a foreigner educated in England. This voice simply told me that if I wanted to see Ruysdale alive again, I should leave my office, say nothing to anyone, leave the hotel, walk a block north on Fifth Avenue, and then east toward Madison. In a bar and grill on the northwest corner of Madison I would find a glassed-in phone booth. I would wait for someone to call in on it. I had, this voice told me, a half an hour, no more."

Chambrun took a cigarette from a lacquered box on the table and lit it. I thought his hands weren't quite steady.

"I wanted to think it was some kind of a crank call," he said. "Everybody in the hotel knew Ruysdale was missing. Somebody trying to be funny? Instinct told me it was for real, so I followed instructions. Tom's Bar and Grill is the name of the place I went to. Took me twenty minutes, I suppose. The minute I reached that public phone booth the phone rang. Too early for me, I thought, but I answered it. It was for me. That told me something, Jerry. I had been watched, followed; the minute I reached that booth someone was signaled and the call made."

"And so, the message?" Jerry said.

"It was the same voice that had made the earlier call," Chambrun said. "He had Ruysdale, he told me. She had been picked up shortly after eleven last night on her way from the hotel to her apartment. She would be all right as long as I did exactly as I was told. She would be released unharmed, he told me, 'provided you do as I tell you, Chambrun, and we don't run into bad luck.' I asked him what kind of bad luck. 'There are always unexpected turns in the road in this kind of venture,' he said. 'It won't be my fault if Miss Ruysdale doesn't make it back to you.' I asked him what he wanted me to do."

"And?..." Jerry Dodd asked. He was impatient for facts.

"It all related to Larry Welch, over there in Penthouse Three," Chambrun told us. "The minute he walked into my office I sensed that he was bad luck. But I owe my life to the man who sent Welch to me."

"And what are you supposed to do?"

"Primarily, nothing," Chambrun said. He punched out his cigarette in a brass ashtray on the table and promptly lit a fresh one. "This charter on the phone knows exactly what our routines are, Jerry. He knows about the phone in the roof car. He knows that anyone who wants to see Welch will have to get Welch's approval over that car phone. What I must *not* do is change that routine in any way. I must *not* add any extra security. I must, above all, *not* let Welch know what is going on. It could frighten him off, send him out of the hotel and into some other hiding place. The man on the phone wants Welch where he is, with nothing changed. 'I know every detail of your operation, Mr. Chambrun. Change anything, and I will be aware of it in a matter of minutes. You will be watched every second, right around the clock. Not just you, but your whole staff.'"

"He suggested we have some kind of rotten apple in our barrel?" Jerry asked.

"It could be, though I doubt it," Chambrun said. "Welch suggested to Mark and me that the man he's investigating had ties with the Middle Eastern world. Now you know, Jerry, that in the last ten years we've had literally hundreds of diplomats from the Arab world, from Israel, from Egypt occupying Penthouse Three. Every one of them would know exactly how our routine works, know the names of the car operators, everything they need to know. It doesn't have to be *our* rotten apple."

"But we have to make sure."

"And risk Ruysdale's safety by having him warned that we are doing something?" Chambrun put out his second cigarette, not half smoked. "This fellow knows at least as much as we know about Welch's plans. A number of important people will come to see him and to examine the evidence he has in that briefcase, which will incriminate someone in a 'high place' in our government. I gather that one of the experts Welch expects is not known to him personally. That man will be intercepted on his way here, and someone will take his place, take over his ID. When that someone gets to Welch he will examine the evidence and if he finds it's incriminating, he will take it, or destroy it, or—if it consists only of duplicates and photostats—force Welch to tell him where the real evidence is hidden. Ten to one, Welch will wind up dead and the murderer will walk out of the hotel without anyone paying the slightest attention to him.''

"And if you warn Welch, Ruysdale will wind up in the morgue!" Jerry said. His dark eyes were blazing with anger.

"That appears to be the scenario," Chambrun said. "If Welch suddenly gets the wind up for some reason and decides to leave the Beaumont, I am to do everything I can do to persuade him that he is safe here and that it would be unwise for him to go somewhere else. If I fail—Ruysdale will pay for that failure."

"And so what do we do?" Jerry asked.

"Nothing," Chambrun said.

"Oh, brother!"

"Until I think of something," Chambrun said.

The man in Penthouse 3 was a sitting duck unless Chambrun chose to sacrifice Betsy Ruysdale to save him. The choice for him was intolerable. Betsy Ruysdale was precious to him, perhaps even more precious than I really knew; and his hotel, his life, his pride, his world, was to be used as a death trap for a man sent to Chambrun for protection by a friend who had once saved his life. Let me say here, parenthetically, that if the threatened man had been the third assistant dishwasher, the choice would have been just as unthinkable to Chambrun. He is a man who, unlike a great part of our so-called civilized society, puts a real value on human life.

Jerry Dodd went off to spread a lie among the people on the hotel staff. Ruysdale had been in touch, was okay, would be gone for a few days. I heard later that Eddie, the bartender in the Trapeze, when he heard the news, announced that the next round of drinks were "on the house."

I stayed with Chambrun in Penthouse 1 in case he thought of something and I could help. He was thinking of Ruysdale.

"She is very important to me, Mark," he said, as if I didn't know. "If anything happens to her, I will hunt down the man responsible and kill him, very slowly, very painfully."

"I know."

He gave me an odd look. "You know that's a dimenovel hero speaking and not an old gentleman who runs a sophisticated 1980s hotel."

"Not so old." I said. I don't really know how old he is.

"I was shooting down Nazi butchers in the back alleys of Paris forty years ago," he said. "I could have done it then without thinking twice. I was a brash idiot then, which was why I got in so much trouble I needed help. I got it—from Claude Perrault. I owe him. If I didn't, I'd have told Larry Welch to take his troubles to the Plaza or the Waldorf Astoria when he came here this morning."

"Perrault probably knows who it is Welch has been investigating," I said. "Would it help to know who that is?"

For the first time that day he managed a frozen smile. "Bless you, Mark," he said. He went to his desk, took a small notebook out of one of the drawers, picked up the phone, and asked for Ora Veach, the chief operator on the switchboard. "I want to make a person-to-person call to Paris, France, Miss Veach, Mr. Claude Perrault." He gave her a number.

Ten minutes later the phone rang. From the look on his face I saw he was disappointed. "You say Madame Perrault is on the wire, Miss Veach? I'll talk to her." He covered the mouthpiece with his hand. "Claude is not there, but his wife—" Then: "Jeanette! *C'est Pierre ici!*" There followed a stream of conversation in French, not a word of which I understood. Eventually he put down the phone and sat still for a moment. "Claude is out of Paris. Business, his wife tells me. He'll be gone for several days and she doesn't know how to reach him."

"That's rather odd for an old gentleman your age, isn't it?" I said.

He gave me a sour look. "Not for Claude. He works for the Sûreté, the department of criminal investigation. He could be following up something for them in South America, for all she knows. When he gets in touch she will tell him I need to talk."

"Madame Perrault couldn't answer your question?"

"She has met Welch, but she had no idea what he is involved in. Claude, she says, never tells her anything that could place her in danger, and she doesn't ask! Claude could be back tonight, tomorrow, next week. She has no idea. 'I will be gone for a few days, *chérie*.' And that could be anything from an hour to a month, she says."

"Well, it was a good idea," I said.

"If Claude gets back in time," he said. He was at the French windows again, looking out across the roof, past Mrs. Haven and her tulips and her Japanese friend, to Penthouse 3. I thought I knew what he was thinking.

"Can't you tell Larry Welch what's happened, warn him?" I asked, after a moment.

Chambrun spun around. "What else do you think I'm trying to figure out?" he asked in that flat, cold voice. "I warn him, he's concerned only for his own hide, and he takes off. Curtains for Ruysdale."

"Would he run if he knew what's at stake?"

"What would you do?" Chambrun said. "What would I do if I was in his shoes? He said there was dynamite in that briefcase, the makings of World War Three. If there's any truth in that, if it isn't just big talk from a swollen-headed journalist, what does he have to consider? Does he stay put, make himself a target so that he can save one life—Ruysdale's—or does he find a safer place and save perhaps thousands of lives?"

"You could protect him and his evidence," I said.

"Then *I* would be sentencing Ruysdale to death," he said. "If that sonofabitch on the telephone knows what he says, he knows about our routines. If someone is sitting right here in the hotel watching, I couldn't add one guard to rooftop security without passing sentence on Ruysdale. I can't do it invisibly." He seemed to freeze. "Or can I?" he said very softly.

I suppose any man who finds himself in big trouble begins searching, subconsciously perhaps, in his mind for where he can get help. Chambrun had more sources than the average man. To begin with, he had a highly efficient and professional security force headed by Jerry Dodd. He couldn't use them if he believed in the threat made by Ruysdale's abductors. He had friends among some of the most influential and important men in the country. He couldn't turn to one of them in case, by some freak of chance, he might be talking to someone involved in Larry Welch's investigation. But there was, apparently, someone he was thinking of as a possible source of help.

"Mark, you remember John Jericho, the artist?" he asked me.

"Big guy, red beard, looks like he could take on the Pittsburgh Steelers single-handed? He drops into the Trapeze now and then."

"He has also been painting pictures of terrorism from one end of the earth to the other," Chambrun said. "He's been sending a message to the rest of the world for some time. Unfortunately no one seems to pay attention. He has a studio in Jefferson Mews down in the Village. I don't have a phone number for him and I hope to God he isn't unlisted. I want you to look him up, go to a public phone, and call him."

"You don't trust the switchboard?"

"At the moment I don't trust anyone," Chambrun said, "except you and Jerry Dodd, and I'm about to trust Jericho." He turned toward the French windows. "And one other person. How to stay invisible in one easy lesson."

"What do I tell Jericho if I reach him?"

"Tell him I asked you to call. Tell him I said, 'Now is the time for all good men...'"

"All good men to what?"

"Just that. 'Now is the time for all good men...' Tell him I'll meet him in the Trapeze whenever he says—but it has got to appear casual, accidental. He mustn't ask for me."

I called Jericho from a public phone booth in the lobby. He was listed. He answered in that deep, hearty voice that went with his size. He remembered me, sounded as if he was really glad to hear from me. I told him I was calling for Chambrun.

"He wants you to meet him in the Trapeze Bar as soon as it's convenient for you," I told him.

"This isn't a good day for me to take time off," he said.

'Chambrun said to tell you 'Now is the time for all good men . . .'"

Jericho's voice seemed to change. "Tell him I'll be there within an hour," he said.

"It's to be casual, as though your meeting was accidental," I said.

He laughed, "Tell him I'll be at the bar getting privately sozzled," he said.

I had no idea what Chambrun had in mind. I didn't trust the house phone, so I went back up to his penthouse in the roof car. When I got there he was sitting on his terrace with Victoria Haven. Toto let me know I wasn't welcome.

"In about an hour," I said to Chambrun.

"Did Pierre tell you I'm about to become famous?" Mrs. Haven asked me.

"Too late," I said. "You're already famous, or at least infamous."

"I adore flattery," Mrs. Haven said.

"Mark, I'd appreciate it if you'd circulate in the lobby," Chambrun said. "Keep an eye on the roof car. If anyone heads up for Larry Welch, don't tell me on the house phone. Just say you've done what I asked you to do."

I took off. On the way down I asked Dick Berger if there'd been any visitors for Penthouse 3.

"Not so far," Dick told me. "That guy's a writer, isn't he? I read an article on him in *Atlantic* on the kidnapping of that American general in Italy some time back. He knew his stuff about that."

"Pretty high-class hotel where the elevator operators reads the *Atlantic*," I said.

"I get my sex life somewhere else," Dick said.

Which reminds me that I have said in some other account of doings at the Beaumont that I have a weakness. I fall in love forever about once every three months. That day I was in love forever for the second week with Hilda Harding, a gorgeous blond singer who was doing a stretch in the Beaumont's nightclub, the Blue Lagoon. I have told myself once or twice that I'm not sure whether it's Hilda or her music I'm in love with. I loathe modern rock. It's about as soothing and attractive to me as a buzz saw outside my window when I'm trying to sleep. Hilda sings old-time standards by Youmans, and Kern, and Berlin, and Rogers and Hammerstein, and Cole Porter, and other greats of the past. Her accompanist, a young gay named Billy Chard, makes magic on the piano, softly, while Hilda creates an equal magic with the old, familiar lyrics. And she is so damned beautiful to look at, standing by the piano. She has the musical skills of Lena Horne, and a body that God must have created in a very good mood. She has an army of followers who don't want to let her out of sight and I didn't dream that first night I heard her that anything would come of my offer to buy her a drink. I got luckier than I could have hoped. She had breakfast with me the next morning in my apartment on the second floor! I was hooked forever—for at least a few months!

Just as I stepped off the roof car at the lobby level I heard Hilda call out my name.

"Mark! You low-down, no-good—" And she was very close to me, gripping the lapels of my jacket. It took courage to resist bending down and kissing her on that lovely mouth in front of a group of gawking Hilda Harding fans plus the usual after-lunch traffic. People hate to go back to work after lunch at the Beaumont. They dawdle awhile before they reluctantly head back for the office. Watching a sort of celebrity like Hilda in action was an excuse for procrastination.

What passed between Hilda and me was personal, intimate, and yet she managed to put on a performance for the rubberneckers. The tips of her fingers touched my jacket, even my cheek. There was an arch, almost flirtatious tilt to her head as she looked up at me. Her quite audible laughter was musical. Just looking at her, I felt stirrings that were not for two-thirty in the afternoon—not on this day, at any rate.

"Have you forgotten that we had a date for luncheon at one o'clock?" Hilda demanded, mock reproach in her voice.

"Oh, brother!" I said.

"'Sister' please," she said. "Not that I feel very sisterly toward you, man."

"I'm so damn sorry," I said. "A crisis of sorts. When my boss says 'fetch,' I fetch."

"You could have called my room, or your room," she said. I knew, and I guess the maid on my floor knew, that there was an enticing black lace negligee hanging in my closet. Forever, yet!

"You can make up for it by buying me an ice coffee in the Trapeze while you have a drink," she said. "I'm due for a rehearsal with Billy Chard in about forty-five minutes. We're putting some new numbers in the act for tonight's show." She slipped her arm through mine. "You have that much time to grovel, my friend."

I couldn't say no. It's even possible I didn't remember that I was supposed to be watching the traffic to and from the roof car. We walked past the gawkers and up the short flight of stairs to the mezzanine and into the Trapeze Bar.

The Trapeze had thinned out after the lunch crush. It's an attractive room. Some artist of the Calder school had decorated it with little mobiles of circus acrobats on trapezes. A faint stirring of air from the air conditioning kept them in constant, gentle motion.

"An ice coffee and a white wine and soda with a twist of lemon," I told Eddie, the bartender, as we aimed for a corner table.

"I caught your show last night, Miss Harding," Eddie said. "You are the greatest!"

"Thank you, sir," she said, and gave him a mock bow.

We settled at the corner table. Her hand reached out under the red-checked tablecloth and covered mine.

"Tell me what your boss told you to fetch," she said. "It must have been something exciting if you can have forgotten all about me. Or have I lost my appeal?"

"You know the story about Adlai Stevenson," I said. "Someone asked him if he didn't think the Reverend Norman Vincent Peale was a modern Saint Paul. Stevenson is supposed to have said, 'I find Peale appalling, and Paul appealing."

"Jokes will get you no place, man," Hilda said.

"Darling, I'm really so sorry," I told her. "Some routines went wrong and I had to check them out. Time went by and I just didn't realize how late it had gotten." The truth was I'd forgotten entirely about the lunch date, with kidnapping and potential murder on my mind. I couldn't tell her that. "When one thing goes wrong in a complex operation like this hotel it's like the domino theory—a dozen other things go wrong. You have to check where the malfunction is, and in a hurry."

She gave my hand a little squeeze. "All right, my love, you are forgiven," she said. "If anything was going to interfere with my making a stage performance on time, I wouldn't remember a lovely lunch date either. I guess everyone's job or profession comes ahead of anything else." Then: "Oh, my!" It was a little cry of amazement. "Do you know what that is?"

I turned to look where she was looking and saw a giant of a man with a bright red beard making for the bar. It was Jericho. He'd done somewhat better than an hour in getting here.

"He's John Jericho, an artist," I said.

"You know him?"

"He's a fairly regular customer. I know him in that way," I said.

At that moment, having ordered his drink, Jericho turned to survey the room, saw me, and waved.

"I've got to meet him!" Hilda said. "He was in my audience one night when I was filling an engagement in Cairo. Have you seen his paintings?"

"Chambrun has one, but he hasn't found a place to hang it," I said. "It's a picture of an Israeli school bus, bombed by terrorists, children blown to pieces, shop windows blown out in the background, a man with his head lying a few yards away. It's not something you want to look at for breakfast—or lunch or dinner for that matter."

"He's marvelous!" Hilda said. "I saw a one-man show of his in Paris. He shows people what's going on in this miserable world. They ought to pass a law that his paintings be hung in every school. Kids would learn what they would have to grow up to stop. I want to meet him, Mark."

Jericho saved me any embarrassment. He came toward our table, carrying a drink. He is, I'd guess, about six feet four and two hundred and forty pounds of suntanned, well-disciplined muscle. He moves with the grace of a dancer. Quite a sight.

"Like some Viking warrior," Hilda said in an awed voice.

Jericho reached us. "Hi, Mark," he said, but he was looking at Hilda, smiling.

I stood up. "This young lady is anxious to meet you," I said. "Hilda Harding, the singer, John Jericho, the painter."

"I don't believe it," Jericho said.

"You heard me sing in Cairo, Mr. Jericho," Hilda said. "Don't you recognize me?"

He shrugged his huge shoulders. "Stage makeup, lights," he said.

"I'm not as pretty as you remember?"

His smile widened. "Prettier," he said. "Now, if you'd sing me a bar or two of 'I Get a Kick Out of You'..."

Hilda pushed back her chair, stood up, and without the slightest hesitation began to sing.

"I get no kick from champagne. Mere alcohol doesn't thrill me at all . . ."

Jericho applauded, as other heads turned our way. Someone shouted out, "Keep going, Hilda!"

"I get paid for singing more than two bars," Hilda called out.

"You are no forgery," Jericho said. "Can I buy you a drink?"

"I have a rehearsal in a few minutes," Hilda said, "but if you'd give me a rain check . . ."

"Anytime anyplace, lady," Jericho said. That's the punch line for an old joke that isn't fit for family consumption. Hilda didn't give any sign that she knew it. She turned to me.

"As long as you have company, Mark, I'll go now—Will you catch one of my turns tonight?"

"You know it," I said.

She turned to leave and there was Chambrun coming into the Trapeze. He didn't seem to see us at all but went to the bar, where he ordered a vermouth on the rocks.

"Shall I tell your boss I waylaid you because I was due an explanation?" Hilda asked.

Jericho put an end to that. He called out in his booming voice, "Hey, Pierre! Long time no see." He crossed over to join Chambrun at the bar. Chambrun showed surprise and pleasure at seeing an old friend.

It was a good act. He appeared not to see Hilda or me as we walked behind them and out of the Trapeze. But I knew he knew I was there and I hadn't been following orders, which was to watch the traffic on the roof car.

By the time Hilda and I reached the lobby I was feeling something more than conscience at having played truant from my assignment for a few minutes. Betsy Ruysdale was not where she should be, for the first time in years. Betsy, so cool and competent and efficient, who would never have let me—or anyone else important to Chambrun—down for even a second, was God knows where, in God knows what kind of circumstances, subjected to God knows what kind of violence or humiliation. Betsy is a resourceful and courageous gal, but she could be scared out of her wits at this moment. One slip by Chambrun or anyone in whom he confided, and Betsy could find herself being shipped home in a trash bag. I had chosen to ignore her and her situation in order to make time with this blond singer who happened to be more than average fun in bed! What a jerk, I told myself!

Hilda went off to her rehearsal and I stood looking around the lobby like some rookie outfielder who has just lost a fly ball in the sun. Had somebody gone up to Penthouse 3 while I held Hilda's hand under the table in the Trapeze? Wouldn't Chambrun have checked himself? He'd know I'd muffed it if he had. Suddenly a strong hand rested on my shoulder and I turned to face a man I was instinctively glad to see. He was Mitchell Prescott, big, broad shouldered, bald as an egg, wearing an expensively tailored tropical worsted blue suit. A shell-briar pipe was clamped between strong white teeth. I don't think I've ever seen Prescott without a pipe. I'd wondered if he'd slept with one pointing toward the ceiling.

"I've been looking for Pierre," he said. "Not in his office, not in his penthouse, no Miss Ruysdale, no you. I'd begun to think I'd wandered into the wrong place."

Prescott is high up in the operation of the CIA, not an undercover type but near the top in the chain of command. He was located officially in Washington, but he keeps a permanent room in the Beaumont. I think a lot of work includes foreign diplomats whose jobs bring them to the United Nations. You could say Prescott was a sort of landmark in the hotel, always just around the corner if you wanted to find him. My instant thought was that he was someone Chambrun would turn to if the going got really tough. Prescott had a skilled army he could call on within seconds of their being needed.

"Something special cooking?" Prescott asked me.

I damn near bit off my tongue to keep from telling him. "Ruysdale's on holiday for a few days," I told him. "The boss is a little like a blind man without his guide dog."

Prescott laughed. "Absence makes the heart grow fonder," he said. "Know where I might find Pierre? I understand the spare penthouse is occupied. We've got a Saudi big shot coming to town in a couple of days and I'd hoped to put him up here."

"I don't know how long the present occupant is booked in for," I said. "We can find a suite for you. We always keep one empty for emergencies."

"The penthouse is so perfect for the special-envoy-type visitor," Prescott said. "Total privacy, except for Victoria's Japanese gentleman friend." He grinned, and tamped down the ashes in the bowl of his pipe with his forefinger. "Seriously, you know where I can locate the boss?"

"Last I knew he was up in the Trapeze having a drink with an old friend."

"Thanks," Prescott said. He held a lighter to his pipe and puffed out a cloud of smoke. "See you around, friend." He headed for the stairway to the mezzanine.

I walked over to the roof car and realized, without looking at my watch, that it was after three o'clock. Dick Berger had been relieved on the car by Bob Ballard. The three shifts run from 7:00 A.M. to 3.00 P.M., three to eleven at night, and Lucky Lewis takes over at eleven till seven in the morning.

"Any callers for Penthouse Three?" I asked Ballard.

"There's someone up there now," Bob told me. "Dick took him up before he went off duty."

"Know who it is?"

Bob shrugged. "Dick cleared him with Mr. Welch. He didn't tell me who. Just said someone had gone up and would, sometime, be coming down."

I started for a house phone to call Larry Welch and ask him if everything was okay. Then I remembered Chambrun hadn't trusted the house phone. We were living in a new world!

The little phone in the roof car gave an irregular ringing sound.

"That's the boss's ring on the second floor," Bob Ballard said. "He's evidently headed up."

"I'll go with you," I said. "I want to see him."

Chambrun was alone when the second-floor door opened. He'd left Jericho behind. He gave me a cold, almost hostile look.

"Prescott find you?" I asked.

"Thanks to you," he said.

"I just wanted to tell you—"

"When we get upstairs," Chambrun said.

Didn't he trust Bob Ballard, for God's sake? When the car door opened at the rooftop level Chambrun spoke to Ballard.

"You know John Jericho by sight, Bob?"

"The artist? Big guy with a red beard?"

"He'll be going back and forth to Mrs. Haven's penthouse for the next few days. He's going to be painting the lady's portrait. Check out with her in the usual way but don't be surprised if you see a lot of Jericho.''

He walked out of the car and under the awning to the front door of his penthouse. There was something rigid about his walk that I have never seen before.

"Jericho's going to be painting Mrs. Haven?'' I asked when we were inside.

He spun around on me, his eyes blazing. "Is it safe to say anything to you without your blabbing it to that blonde when she gets you in the hay?'' he asked.

"Look, I'm sorry, boss. I had a lunch date with her. With all that's going on I didn't call her to tell her I couldn't keep it. She flagged me in the lobby and I had to take time to explain.''

"To tell her that Ruysdale's been kidnapped, that Larry Welch's life is in danger?''

"Of course not. I just told her something had gone wrong with regular routines and you'd asked me to check.''

He sat down in the chair by the French windows. Again there was that unaccustomed gesture of covering his face with his hands.

"Welch has a visitor,'' I told him. "Dick Berger cleared it with him before he went off duty. I don't know who it is. I'm sorry I blew it. You want me to wander over there?''

He lowered his hands, and I saw the stricken look to his face. "No, I don't want you to wander over there." If he'd slapped me, I couldn't have been more aware of his anger. Goddamn it, Mark, if I can't trust you! . . ."

I just stood there waiting for him to let it all out. "I'm sorry," he said after a moment. "The whole damn thing is like juggling a hot coal. The smallest misstep, one careless word to someone and—and Ruysdale could be dead and Welch in mortal danger."

"I haven't said anything to anyone that could put anyone on the spot. Not even Jericho, or Prescott, your friends."

"There are four people now besides me who know what's going on," he said. "You, Jerry Dodd, Jericho, and Victoria Haven."

"You told them?"

"And may regret it for the rest of my life if somebody smells a rat," he said. He snapped open his silver case and took out one of his Egyptian cigarettes. His hands weren't quite steady as he held his lighter to it. "The only way to protect Welch and at the same time not endanger Ruysdale was to do it invisibly, I told you. To manage that I had to get Jericho to agree to help. He's a man who's devoted his life to fighting violence. He's going to paint Victoria. He'll be on the roof constantly for as long as this situation lasts. He'll be visible, but his real reason for being there will be invisible. He knows the kind of people Welch may be involved with. He'll see everybody who comes and goes."

"The boys on the roof car can fill you in if Jericho doesn't know someone," I said.

"God help me, I can't trust anyone without telling them everything," Chambrun said. "If I ask too many questions, one of the car operators may wonder, out loud, why I'm so particularly interested in Larry Welch. Tell me about Prescott."

"Nothing to tell. He had been looking for you, couldn't find you. Went up to the office and discovered Ruysdale was missing. He said he was interested in Penthouse Three for some Saudi diplomat."

"What did you tell him?"

"That Ruysdale was taking a few days' vacation and that you were lost without her. That I didn't know how long the present occupant of Penthouse Three was staying, but that we could find a suite for his Saudi friend. I'm afraid I did tell him you were in the Trapeze with a friend."

"I can read your mind, Mark. You were thinking Prescott is someone who might help us."

"Well—yes, I did."

"Mark, Mark, Mark! Cops, and even supercops like Prescott, solve crimes *after they've been committed!* If, as I was warned, there is someone watching every move I make, all I have to do is been seen *talking* to Prescott and they may decide I'm taking some kind of counteraction. Damn it, Mark, Ruysdale's out there somewhere, hanging by her fingernails!''

"I'm sorry. I hadn't thought—"

"Well, *think* from now on, man." He snuffed out his half-smoked cigarette. "I had just enough time to alert Jericho and pull it off for Prescott. Big deal. I was arranging to have a famous lady, my friend, have a portrait painted by a famous artist, my friend. Jericho's gone home to collect his painting materials. He'll be up here, on guard, in about an hour."

"He's really going to paint Mrs. Haven?"

"Of course. We can't risk anything but the real thing. Now, at five o'clock Victoria will make her usual trip down to the Trapeze for cocktails. Jericho will be with her. I want you there to help spread the word that the lady is about to become immortal. Get it to the press. Buy drinks for anyone you think may spread the word. It has to be known that this has been long planned—long before what's happened here today. The people who have Ruysdale may wonder if this is what it really is. They have to believe this is something I can't change without having to answer difficult questions. The truth has to stay invisible, Mark. I count on you."

THERE IS no place like a busy hotel, especially at the eating, drinking, and entertainment times of the day and night, to watch someone, spy on someone who is circulating in that hotel world. You don't need a passport to get through the front door. You won't stand out just because you aren't a regular customer. Hundreds of people who have never been there before pass through the lobby every day, dine or lunch in the grill or the main dining room, drink in the bars, shop in the specialty places and boutiques in the lobby arcade. You don't attract attention from our security people just because you are a stranger, unless of course you act peculiarly or suspiciously. Ruysdale's kidnappers, with their sights aimed at Larry Welch, could be in the hotel in droves and not attract attention. They'd be just part of the daily influx of strangers. Strangers are as much a part of our business as the literally thousands of registered guests and daily customers. You could be "invisible" here right out in the open—except for the roof level.

There could be a bomb threat—and we've had them—or the rumor of a high-class hotel thief on the loose, and immediately Jerry Dodd and some forty security men would be alerted, plus bellboys, captains and headwaiters in the restaurants and bars, maintenance people, doormen, shopkeepers, room service waiters, an army on the lookout for trouble. In this situation, the threat of a possible double murder, there were just five of us who knew the score. Three of us could circulate, looking for God knows what or who—Chambrun, Jerry Dodd, and me. Jericho and Mrs. Haven would be anchored on the roof. All of us were committed to a kind of deadly silence. To talk to anyone might result in some small action that could trigger a disaster. To take one step outside of what was a daily routine could make a killer, or killers, dangerously nervous. And someone, whom we couldn't identify yet, knew those routines and could report the moment we deviated from them.

I don't mind saying that it was a terrifying situation. I found myself almost afraid to look at people—people I knew and people I didn't know. Too much interest in a stranger might sound an alarm. It was almost worse with people I knew—the staff, regular customers. How did I usually react to them? What kind of a smile did I usually give them? Was there some little joke that we usually exchanged? I don't think I have a professional smile or manner. I am just myself, normally courteous to casual acquaintances and guests, a ready insult or gibe for people I knew well. It wasn't planned, it was just instinctive. Suddenly every contact involved a hidden tension. How did I usually play it with this particular man or woman? If I overplayed it, would they suspect something? If I underplayed it, what then? Was someone I'd always trusted and liked the enemy? I suddenly felt as if I were walking on explosive eggs. The lobby, the bars, even my office and Chambrun's were all at once hostile places. Someone was watching, waiting for me to make some kind of suspicious move. I would have given anything that late afternoon if I hadn't known what was cooking, if I hadn't had to be on guard against some foolish slip.

But, as five o'clock approached, I left my office. First I tried out Chambrun's scenario on my office girl and secretary, Shelda Mason. Once upon a time, long ago, I'd been in love with Shelda Mason forever. She'd withstood the tragedy of losing me and stayed on as an extremely efficient helper.

"Big doings in the Trapeze," I told her. "Mrs. Haven is going to have her picture painted."

"A little late, isn't it?" Shelda said.

"What's important is who's doing the painting," I said. "John Jericho."

Shelda grinned at me. "Well, he paints battlefields, doesn't he? Now, if the old lady was fifty years younger, that might be a juicy item. You want me to do something with it, Mark? A press release?"

I tried to make it sound causal. "Jericho's wanted her to sit for him for a long time and she's finally agreed. It's a story. He turned down the president of the United States once. Any picture he paints runs into six figures at today's prices."

"Why the old lady? Are they friends?"

"The glamour girl of the century," I said.

Shelda was, without knowing it, asking me the right questions, questions I'd have to answer in a few minutes in the Trapeze.

"It could give the gossip columnists a chance to revive the story of her life," Shelda said. "I've heard she had famous lovers who died long before I was born. My grandmother will enjoy reading about those old romances. An artist painting a picture of an old lady isn't much of a story. But if we could remind people that she had a love affair with Calvin Coolidge—"

"Coolidge? Never!"

"Well, I was just picking a name out of the hat," Shelda said. "You have to give it some spice, Mark." She gave me a sly look. "I've heard it rumored that the lady and Chambrun were once an older woman-younger man thing."

"I wouldn't know," I said, though I'd heard the rumor, too.

"He lets her keep a dog in the hotel," Shelda said. "That could be a symptom of real love."

"You've got a superimagination," I said.

She gave me a Mona Lisa smile. "I was taught by a master," she said.

Why had I fallen out of love with Shelda, I asked myself. She had been a lot of fun back then.

Victoria Haven—tall, erect, moving with astonishing grace and vigor for her age—made a daily "entrance" into the Trapeze Bar every afternoon at five. You could tell time by her. Carrying Toto under one arm and Toto's red satin cushion under the other, she would cross the room, smiling and nodding to familiar people, to the corner table always reserved for her.

Today something was added, a giant, red-bearded escort who instantly caught the attention of the women customers in the bar. I was just in time, coming from the rear door, to see them make their way across the room. The room was moderately populated for the event. In another half hour it would be crowded with people coming out of work. Mrs. Haven has told me, straight-facedly, that she came ahead of the crowd to avoid attracting attention. As if attracting attention hadn't been her whole life! She and Jericho and Toto, enthroned on his cushion, made quite a picture at the corner table.

Looking around the room, I saw a lot of people I knew by sight, including Mitch Prescott, who was standing at the bar nursing his pipe and smiling as he watched the parade to the corner table. A woman's voice called out my name and I saw Martha Madden, the syndicated gossip columnist, sitting alone. Martha belongs to the almost forgotten school of Hedda Hopper—hat, jewelry, cigarettes in a long ivory holder, and, of all things, a lorgnette worn around her neck on a gold chain. Martha wouldn't have been caught dead in an ordinary pair of glasses. People in films and theater and the world of arts saw her appear where they were with mixed emotions. She had the power to give their careers an enormous lift if she liked them, and she could strike a mortal blow to their vital organs if she didn't. Americans are eager to hear the "dirt" about famous people, and Martha had gotten rich and famous dishing it out. I knew she hadn't come to have a drink all by herself at the

Beaumont without a professional reason. I guessed that Chambrun must have tipped her off that there would be a story.

"Do sit down, Mark," Martha said. "I don't like to be seen in public alone." She was drinking a dry martini in a chilled glass. "Chambrun rarely gives me a bad tip, but I must say I don't see why I should be interested in that grotesque parade of man, woman, and dog."

"Famous and very great old lady and one of the outstanding artists of our time embarked on a venture together," I said.

"Pierre told me that on the phone. Why did he want me here? I owe him favors, so I came, but it's not gossip, Mark, which is my business."

I smiled at her and told a hovering waiter that I, too, would have a dry martini in a chilled glass. "I just heard today that Victoria Haven may have had an affair with Calvin Coolidge," I said.

She lifted her lorgnette and looked at me like a scientist might examine a bug under a microscope. "You have to be kidding," she said. "Silent Cal would never have known how to ask!"

"Sign language," I suggested. "Seriously, that old gal could probably give you more gossip about famous men of the last sixty years than you could dream of. Fill your space those days when there isn't anything very hot cooking. Since she is about to be made immortal by John Jericho, I guess the boss thought you might find her in a mood to remember some choice items."

"I wouldn't have come at all," Martha said, "If I hadn't needed help from Pierre on something else. One of my so called reliable sources tells me that Larry Welch is here at the Beaumont. I've tried to call him on the phone, but your switchboard won't put me through directly to him and he won't accept a call from me."

It was like being suddenly shocked by a live wire. Larry Welch was what this whole charade was about, but Martha Madden, of all people, wasn't supposed to make the connection. Give her the slightest hint, and she could turn a searchlight on what Chambrun was so desperately trying to keep invisible.

"You know Larry?" Martha asked me.

"Met him, when he's stayed here from time to time," I said. As far as I knew, Larry Welch had never stayed at the Beaumont before.

"My source tells me he's involved in a really big story," Martha said. "He wouldn't make himself so inaccessible if he wasn't. Where is he, in the bridal suite?"

I didn't even want to mention the roof, or she would be trying to find a way to get up there herself.

"I asked your Mr. Atterbury at the front desk and he tells me Larry isn't registered, but your switchboard sings a different song. 'I'll see if Mr. Welch can accept your call.' And then: 'I'm sorry, but Mr. Welch can't take your call at this time.' Your people ought to get their signals straight."

"A lot of famous people stay here who don't register at the front desk," I said. I grinned at her. "That's to keep reporters like you from making their lives miserable. They register in Chambrun's office. Atterbury probably told you the truth, and ditto the switchboard."

"Tell Pierre I want to get to Larry Welch, and that I count on him to arrange it," Martha said. Her lorgnette was now focused on Victoria Haven's table. "That old crone seems to attract men like a burlesque queen about to do a striptease."

It was true. About a dozen gentlemen had gathered around the table getting the charm treatment from Victoria and what Eddie, the bartender, has called "the B.C. treatment" from Toto. B.C. for "beneath contempt!"

"Sixty years ago the line would have been around the block," I told Martha.

"What has she got that I haven't got?" Martha asked.

"She doesn't bite or sting," I said.

"Look at Mitch Prescott, over there at the bar, watching her and grinning like a Cheshire cat!" Martha said. "I've done that supercop a dozen important favors in my time. Is he over here saying hello to me? That sideshow over there has got him hooked!"

"I'm afraid I've got to join it," I said. "It's part of my job to help spread the word that John Jericho is abandoning his crusade against world violence to paint a very gracious lady."

As I stood up to leave, Martha's fingers, strong as piano wires, closed on my wrist. "Tell Pierre if he doesn't get me to Larry Welch, I just might take a few random shots at his beloved hotel."

I was still forcing a smile. "I ought to warn you, luv, that a war with Chambrun is one you could lose, in spite of your column in umpteen hundred newspapers."

"I know you get paid to protect Chambrun," she said, "so I forgive you for that one. All I want is for him to get Welch to talk to me on the phone. Once I've got Welch listening I'll take my own chances on the next move."

As I crossed toward Victoria Haven's table Mich Prescott joined me. He was filling a pipe from a brightly colored roll-up pouch.

"Extraordinary woman," he said. He was talking about Mrs. Haven. "Approaching age scares the hell out of some of us. I'm thirty years younger than Victoria and I'm already wondering how much farther the road goes. I get winded if I walk across town too briskly—I wonder if this pipe is going to give me throat cancer. When I look at a handsome woman I wonder if the time is coming when I might not be able to make it. Victoria? She's spent her life attracting men and at eighty she's still competition for today's glamour girls.''

"It's an art," I said.

Prescott held a lighter to his pipe. "I hope Jericho has the sense to give his painting to the Beaumont, and that Chambrun will have the sense to hang it in the Trapeze so that she'll be here with her friends forever.''

"I suspect she'll outlast the lot of us," I said.

His strong white teeth bit down on the stem of his pipe. "You could be right, you know," he said.

The gathering around Victoria's table was not all centered on her. Jericho was getting his share of attention. What did he think about Israel's war against the PLO? What did he think about the IRA bombing in London that had killed men and horses in a routine changing of the guard? Was Armageddon around the corner? Jericho fought off these serious questions with his bright smile.

"An artist has to change his perspective from time to time," he told his audience. "I've been concentrating for a long time on violence and death. I'm turning now to beauty and life for a change of pace."

"Too late, I'm afraid," Victoria said.

"You only look at yourself in the mirror, my sweet," Jericho said. "You don't light up for yourself. But for us your real beauty comes from an inner something. If I can catch that, I'll produce a masterpiece. That's why I'm going to have to spend the next few days with you, round the clock, so that I don't miss any glimpse of that inner excitement there is to catch."

"Fifty years ago I wouldn't have given you time to paint me," Victoria said.

"Fifty years ago I wasn't even a gleam in my father's eyes," Jericho said, "My misfortune. But who knows, lovely lady, who knows?"

"There's a lady across the room who can gossip about us," Victoria said.

"She'll have to guess at it," Jericho said, "because you and I are going to have a very private time together." He smiled at the army around the table. "If Victoria doesn't show up for a few days, don't worry about her. If I get lucky, she'll be having fun!"

It was very neatly played. No one gathered around the table could have guessed that Victoria Haven's absence from her regular five o'clock routine for the next few days represented anything but a famous artist having persuaded her to give him her undivided attention.

Mitch Prescott was tugging at my sleeve.

"Can you leave the world of budding romance for a moment," he asked. Something about his voice made me turn to give him a quick look. "Over there at the bar," he said. "The man with the dark sunglasses."

Standing apart from a half dozen other drinkers was a tall, wiry-looking man with very black, patent-leather-looking hair. He had a tan that suggested he'd spent a lot of time at a beach somewhere. He was staring down, through black lenses, at a drink that didn't seem to interest him. Neither did the gay gathering around Victoria Haven and Jericho seem to be of any interest to him.

"What about him?" he asked.

"I never saw him before in my life," I said. "He's not a regular, that much I know."

Prescott was frowning. "I know him from somewhere," he said. "My kind of business must not be unlike yours, Mark. You see hundreds of faces every day, people you've never seen before. Run into one of them out of your usual environment and you can't place them, but they're familiar."

"That one looks like George Raft in an old Warner Brothers gangster movie," I said.

"I guess I'm getting old," Prescott said. "Everyone looks like someone I've seen in all the criminal mug shots I have looked at. I could swear that guy— would you mind asking Eddie about him, Mark? If I ask him, he'll freeze. I'm a good customer, but the minute I start asking questions I'm a cop."

What Prescott couldn't know was that any reason to suspect a stranger in the Beaumont was vital at the moment. Chambrun had been warned that we were watched, that any deviation from normal routines would be instantly noticed, reported, and Betsy Ruysdale would suffer the consequences. Chambrun didn't want to believe that anyone on his staff would have sold us out, but who else could be so familiar with routines? Any regular customer was the answer; any one of literally hundreds of diplomats who had stayed in Penthouse 3. I've seen them come and go over the years, white men, black men, brown-skinned Arabs, Orientals. This character with the black glasses and the patent-leather hair could have been one of them, his appearance altered for his present purposes. If Prescott felt some vague doubts about him, I should check him out.

I left Prescott and walked over to the far end of the bar. Eddie came over to me after he'd finished making a batch of cocktails for a group at the other end of the mahogany.

"Madame Victoria seems to be having a ball," he said.

"The guy with the black glasses, you know who he is, Eddie?"

Eddie shrugged. "Been around for the last few days around this time," Eddie said.

"He registered here?" I asked.

"Hell, Mark, you don't have to have a passport to buy a drink here. He isn't talkative, I didn't ask him."

"You don't recognize him from some other time?"

Eddie shook his head. "I would remember, too," he said. "When I say 'a drink'—that one nurses one vodka and tonic longer than it takes the average woman to have a baby! That kind of customer I'd remember. No tips!''

"Keep looking my way," I said. "I don't want him to guess we're talking about him. Prescott thinks he's seen him before somewhere, maybe in a mug shot.''

Eddie grinned. "Mitch sees an international crook in anyone whose name and social security number he doesn't know. This guy just seems to be killing time between dates. He doesn't appear to be waiting for anyone, unless it's a train back to the suburbs. He's come in the last four afternoons, just before Mrs. Haven's entrance, and left in less than an hour. One drink!''

It could mean something, probably meant nothing. A guy just killing time in a pleasant place. I was just about to report back to Prescott when one of the regular bellhops came up to me.

"Mr. Chambrun wants you up in his penthouse, Mr. Haskell. On the double is the word.''

I went down to the lobby and across to the elevators. Somewhat to my surprise, Johnny Thacker, the day bell captain, was operating the roof car instead of Bob Ballard. He signaled Chambrun's phone, told him I was on the way up.

"Something screwy going on here," Johnny said. "The guy in Penthouse Three called the switchboard to say he had a guest in the lobby who wanted to come up and this roof car didn't respond. I checked it out. According to the indicator, the car was stopped at the

tenth floor. None of the regular operators stop anywhere between the lobby, the second floor, and the
roof—unless it's Chambrun, or you, or Jerry Dodd,
someone with authority to tell them to stop."

"So what does Bob Ballard say?"

"He doesn't say anything because we haven't been
able to find him. The car was stopped at ten, empty,
no Bob. I figure he must have got sick and had to get
to the john in a hurry. There was nothing mechani-
cally wrong with the car. It was just deserted."

"And the passenger for Penthouse Three?"

"Oh, I took him up, eventually. Guy in a tizzy because he'd been kept waiting for half an hour. I was
ordered by Chambrun to take over the car until Bob
shows up or we can get the night operator to come on
early."

"It's not like Bob to just duck out," I said.

"You know that," Johnny said. "Jerry Dodd's got
people looking for him. He could be sick or hurt."

It turned out that Bob Ballard was a great deal
worse than sick or hurt. One of Jerry Dodd's men
found his body stuffed into a metal trash can on the
tenth floor, outside the rear service elevator. The top
of his head had been blown away by three heavy-duty
slugs from some kind of a magnum handgun.

Part Two

ONE

JOHNNY THACKER, running the roof car in place of Bob Ballard, hadn't known what I found out from Chambrun when I entered the penthouse. Just minutes before, one of Jerry Dodd's men had made the gruesome discovery on the tenth floor. He hadn't been looking for anything but a sick young man somewhere. The lid to the trash can in the service area hadn't been fitted on properly. A simple instinct for neatness, ingrained into every Beaumont employee, prompted this security guy—his name was Barnhardt—to try to close the lid the way it should be. It wouldn't close as it should and Barnhardt lifted the lid off to see what was blocking it. He found himself looking down into the obliterated face of a dead man.

Barnhardt acted with the kind of efficiency for which we were normally proud at the Beaumont. He tried to locate Jerry Dodd on the service phone right there by the trash can, put out an alarm for Jerry, and, without ever leaving Bob Ballard's dead body, called the police. You didn't have to be a trained security guard to recognize this as a homicide. Barnhardt then tried to locate Chambrun in his office and, failing that, called Penthouse 1. Chambrun was just putting down the phone as I walked into his living room. He looked at me as if I were a total stranger.

"You sent for me," I said when he didn't speak.

"Barnhardt couldn't locate Jerry, so he's called the police," Chambrun said, in a dead-sounding voice. "It was the right thing for him to do. He had no way of knowing that we are facing any kind of special situation. We're going to be swarming with cops and I have no way to stop it."

"Stop it?"

"There should be no change in our routines. That's the price we pay for Ruysdale's safe return. The police are going to turn those routines upside down." He glanced at his watch. "Just six o'clock," Chambrun said. "You were in the Trapeze when Victoria and Jericho turned up there at five. Did they indicate there was anything out of the ordinary when they made their trip down from the roof?"

"No conversation about it at all," I said. "Everything seems to be going the way you wanted it to down there. Regular customers all know about the painting. Martha Madden is there, thanks to you. How did everyone know Ballard was missing? You had people looking for him."

"Someone calling to see Larry Welch. No car to bring him up here. Car was stopped at ten. That was the obvious place to start looking for Ballard, who wasn't where he should be. Johnny Thacker took over the car and brought Welch's guest up."

"Brought me up, too," I said. "Five minutes ago he didn't know what had happened to Ballard."

"There's no way not to let Welch know what's happened," Chambrun said. "If we don't, the police will. He gets the wind up, decides to move somewhere else, and Ruysdale's had it."

"Look," I said. "Welch is a tough guy, used to tough situations. I'll bet if you tell him what's cooking, he'll play along with you."

"Or he'll just say he's sorry, can't risk it, and take off," Chambrun said. "According to him, he has more at stake than his own safety." He brought his fist down on the table beside his chair. "You're going to have to handle this for me, Mark. What has the traffic been to Penthouse Three? We know Johnny Thacker just took someone up there. But before that, who went up, when did they come down? Who last rode an uninterrupted trip with Bob Ballard? Someone from Penthouse Three? Victoria and Jericho? I'll check in the Trapeze. You go across the roof and talk to Welch. He knows Ballard was missing from the car when his present guest arrived. Just tell him Ballard is still missing. No more than that. I need time to think about telling him anything else."

I walked across the roof, past Mrs. Haven's deserted quarters, and to Penthouse 3. I knocked on the front door. Nothing happened until I knocked a second time, loud and hard. The door opened and Larry

Welch, looking unfriendly, opened up. When he saw me he gave me his Burt Reynolds smile.

"Hi, Mark," he said. "I'm tied up at the moment. If you could come back later? . . ."

"Just a quick question," I said. "The guy who was operating the roof car is still missing. I'm trying to find out who saw him last. I mean, if Bob Ballard said anything about being sick, or something like that."

"I never did see him," Larry said. "He brought up an early caller I had, took him down later."

"When was that?"

"Oh boy, let me see. It was Martin Stearns. State Department character. He arrived before two, left a little after five, I guess."

After five; that would have been after Victoria Haven and Jericho had gone down to the Trapeze.

"Your Mr. Stearns didn't have any trouble getting a ride down?" I asked.

Larry shrugged. "He'd have come back here if there hadn't been any ride down," he said. "My present caller is the one who had the trouble. No ride up. He called me on the house phone to say the roof car wasn't operating. I called your security man, Dodd, and he said he'd have someone on the car in a few minutes. It took nearly twenty minutes or more, but my caller is here. And now if you'll excuse me, Mark—"

"Is there some way I can reach this Stearns guy to ask him about his ride down?"

"I don't know if he's staying overnight in town," Larry said. "Washington is his base. I suppose some-one at the State Department might tell you where he's staying in New York, if he is staying. He could be fly-ing back to Washington right now, I suppose."

"You didn't have to be in touch with him again?"

"No. I'm sorry, Mark. I can't help you and I've got to get back to my caller."

"There's been nobody else? Just Stearns and the person who's with you now?"

"Nobody. And now—see you later."

One small fact clicked into place as I walked back across the roof to Chambrun's penthouse. If this Martin Stearns had arrived a little before two, Dick Berger had been operating the roof car, would have had to clear him with Welch before he took him up. But at three o'clock Bob Ballard relieved Dick, so Bob would have been on the down trip a little after five. I didn't think that added up to much of anything at the time. But I filed it away.

Just as I was approaching Chambrun's place the roof elevator disgorged some passengers—Cham-brun, Mrs. Haven, and Jericho. Johnny Thacker was still running the car and it wasn't until he headed down that I realized Chambrun hadn't as yet told Mrs. Ha-ven and Jericho what had happened.

"I just don't believe it!" I heard Mrs. Haven say.

We all trooped into Chambrun's living room. Everyone seemed to want to talk at once, but Chambrun kept command of the moment.

"Police are going to be here any minute," he said.

"And you don't want them told about Miss Ruysdale?" Jericho asked.

"Until I know more, John," Chambrun said. His voice sounded hoarse. "There's an outside chance this violence has nothing to do with the kidnapping. It could be something in Ballard's life, something totally unrelated. Until I'm sure, I can't risk blowing the ball game."

"You know you don't believe it's unrelated," Jericho said. "You don't believe in coincidences any more than I do."

"Why would he leave the car at the tenth floor?" Mrs. Haven asked.

"Someone blew his head off with a gun," Chambrun said. "That was enough weapon to get him to stop the car and get off at ten."

"But *why?*" Mrs. Haven persisted.

"That, my dear Victoria, is the jackpot question," Chambrun said.

Mrs. Haven bent down and set Toto loose. The little spaniel gave us a nasty look, went over to the screen door to the terrace, and waited for someone to open it for him. Jericho obliged him and got a small snarl for his pains. They were going to be interesting companions in Penthouse 2, I thought.

"Ballard was such a nice young man," Mrs. Haven was saying to Chambrun. "Always courteous, always helpful. He and the other two, Lucky and Dick, have helped to make me feel as safe as an old lady with a trunkful of jewelry in her bedroom can feel in this vicious city."

"A wife and two young kids," Chambrun said. He glanced at me. "Someone's going to have to tell them." He turned to Victoria Haven. "I asked you and Jericho to help me in a very difficult situation, Victoria. In view of what's happened, if you don't want to go on with it..."

"You don't think young Mr. Welch is still in danger?" Mrs. Haven asked him.

"I have no way of knowing whether anything has changed," Chambrun said. "Danger to Welch, I mean. But police are going to be crawling all over the place unless there's a quick solution to Ballard's murder. That will surely interfere with the kidnappers' plans, whatever they are."

"We have to do what we can for Ruysdale," Mrs. Haven said. "She's our friend, our cherished friend. If you still want Jericho up here to watch things, I'm quite willing to provide him with an excuse." She gave Jericho a dazzling smile. "Besides, he says he's really going to paint me, in case someone should look over his shoulder. I can't resist that, Pierre."

"Things have been moving so fast," I heard myself say, "I've never gotten around to asking you a ques-

tion, boss. Larry Welch is in danger. You can't tell him
how you know because it might scare him off and that
could cost Betsy Ruysdale. So you dream up a scheme
to plant Jericho here on the roof to protect Welch if
necessary. If it becomes necessary, and Jericho fouls
up whatever these creeps have in mind for Welch,
won't that be just as bad for Ruysdale?"

"If they believe I'm up here to paint Mrs. Haven,"
Jericho said, "then if and when I get in the act I will
just have been standing on the street corner, minding
my own business, waiting for a bus, when I spotted
some kind of trouble." He gave me a sardonic little
smile. "And Pierre's conscience will be clear. He will
have protected a hotel guest he knew was in danger
without putting Ruysdale on the spot."

"And you're willing to be a sitting duck for a guy
armed with a magnum handgun who's now demon-
strated he's willing and able to use it? Why?" I asked.

Jericho's face hardened under his bright red beard.
"Because Betsy Ruysdale is an old friend, a friend of
friends, and because I hate violence and I hope to get
the sonofabitch who's responsible for harming her."

"Violently?" I said.

He grinned at me. "When I'm violent it's justice.
When someone else is violent it's a crime against society."

"Getting Ruysdale back safe is all that matters at
the moment," Chambrun said.

"But you'll still protect Larry Welch, which is the one thing Ruysdale's kidnapper told you you mustn't do?" I asked.

Chambrun never got to answer that question. The phone on his desk rang and he reached for it and answered. He listened for a moment and then said, "On my way."

He put down the phone. "That was Jerry Dodd," he said. "The police are on the tenth floor. I'm needed there. You, too, Mark; decisions will have to be made about what the press are to be told."

"Don't worry about up here, Pierre," Jericho said. "Mrs. Haven and Toto and I will keep an eye on Welch."

"Don't joke about Toto," Chambrun said. "That little pooch may be more valuable than you think. He doesn't like strangers and he'll let you know, loud and clear."

THE BEAUMONT is like a city within a city. We have our own mayor, Chambrun; our own police force, headed by Jerry Dodd; restaurants, bars, shops, the branch office of a big bank; a hospital, headed by Dr. Partridge, our house physician. Like any big city, our population ranges from decent, honest, hard-working citizens, to crooks and con men, whores and pimps, pickpockets, thieves, and big-time criminals. Chambrun and his staff manage this variety better than most city governments, but you can't totally eliminate human impulses toward greed, revenge, and violence. They are unhappy components of what I've come to believe is a sick society.

Bob Ballard's death is not the first murder that has happened in the Beaumont. I remember Chambrun saying once that the Lord seems to lean just a little on the side of "the good guys." There was, he thought, always a piece of luck that went his way. That early August evening the first piece of good luck came our way. The Homicide man sent from police headquarters to handle the Ballard case was Lieutenant Walter Hardy. You could say Hardy is an old friend. He's been involved in crimes at the Beaumont before this. Hardy works in the precinct in which the Beaumont is located, so it isn't pure chance that we got him this time. He could have been involved on another case, but he wasn't.

This was good luck because Hardy and Chambrun trust each other. Chambrun works with a kind of intuitive brilliance on a case; Hardy is a slow, plodding, check-every-detail kind of a cop. A big blond man, he looks more like a professional football linebacker than a skilled, expertly trained detective. He and Chambrun make a great team; Chambrun comes up with a magical guess, and Hardy puts together the puzzle, piece by piece, so that the district attorney will have a case in court. In the tricky situation in which Chambrun found himself at the moment, Hardy could be a blessing.

Johnny Thacker was still running the roof car when we went down to ten. He wasn't the same young man who'd brought me up a little while ago.

"God, I grew up with Bob," he told us. "Played on the same stickball team with him when we were six! Look, Mr. Chambrun, when I can get off I'd like to go be with Bob's wife, Anne, and their kids."

"You know of any personal problems he had?" Chambrun asked. "Trouble with anyone on the staff?"

"One of the most popular guys working here," Johnny said. "You know that, Mr. Chambrun."

"I know," Chambrun said.

The car stopped at ten.

"I figure he must have seen someone on our black-list snooping around where he shouldn't be," Johnny said. "Get my hands on him, and so help me . . ."

Johnny opened the car door.

"As soon as Hardy's talked to you, Johnny, get someone else to take over the car till Lucky gets here, and go to Anne. Tell her I'll see her as soon as I can get free. She's not to worry—about money, or arrangements, or anything." Chambrun's mouth was a thin slit. "What else can I say to her?"

There were cops everywhere on ten, knocking on room doors trying to find guests who might have seen or heard something. Chambrun and I walked down the hall to the rear service area. There was really a crowd there: police photographers, men dusting for fingerprints. There was also Lieutenant Hardy.

"I'd like to meet you sometime, Pierre, just for a drink and maybe talk about baseball," the lieutenant said to Chambrun. He glanced at the iron trash barrel. "He's still there, but you don't have to look. Spoil your appetite for dinner. He's been officially identified by the man who found him."

I saw Barnhardt, Jerry Dodd's man, standing off to one side looking as though he were seasick.

"Weapon?" Chambrun asked.

"Is there ever one when you want it?" Hardy said. "We won't have a ballistics report until the medical examiner gets here and lets us move him. At least three shots to the head. Looks like some kind of a magnum gun. We don't have to talk here, Pierre, but I need facts about him from you—or someone."

"Ask me," Chambrun said in the flat, dead voice he'd acquired since that morning, when Betsy Ruysdale didn't come to work. "You're needed here. I've been around dead people before. I run a hotel. People live here and die here."

"But not so often with three slugs right through the forehead," Hardy said. He took a notebook out of his pocket. "I got some kind of a poop sheet on him from Jerry Dodd. 'Robert Alden Ballard, aged twenty-nine; married to Anne Gerber Ballard; two kids, Richard five, Marilyn three. Born and raised in the Bronx. High school, college, army, honorable discharge, and a job in Washington, D.C. Came to work for you about two years ago.' I see he's been getting five hundred bucks a week. That's pretty good for an elevator operator, isn't it?"

"Special job, special pay," Chambrun said. "The three men who run that roof car are really part of our security force. They help protect important diplomats from all over the world."

"Plus Mrs. Haven and you," Hardy said.

"Coincidentally," Chambrun said.

"So how does he qualify for that job? You'd think it would go to someone who'd been with you a long time, earned your trust. Been here only two years, according to my notes."

"Combination of circumstances, as I recall," Chambrun said. "A regular guest here at the Beaumont is Mike Dent. United States Secret Service, travels with and guards important foreign dignitaries. Just in passing one day he told me about a young man in Washington, army-intelligence background, anxious to get back to New York, where his roots were. Jobs were hard to come by. Could I use him? As a favor to a friend, I interviewed him, had him checked out, hired him. It so happened we needed a man for roof security, rather special job. He qualified. There was no one waiting in line for the job. One other thing that helped me make up my mind—he'd grown up with Johnny Thacker, my day bell captain. Johnny couldn't say enough for him. That did it."

"I understand you have three men on that job in eight-hour shifts," Hardy said. "Ballard's shift was from three in the afternoon to eleven at night. He'd only been on two, three hours today when this happened."

"This much I can tell you," Chambrun said. "Shortly before five o'clock he took Mrs. Haven and John Jericho, who was with her, down to the lobby. No problems. Not too long after that he took down a guest who was visiting the occupant of Penthouse Three."

"And no problems?"

"I can't answer that with the facts at hand," Chambrun said. "The guest was Martin Stearns, State Department, I understand. He was taken up to call on Larry Welch, who's in Penthouse Three, by Dick Berger, who has the shift before Ballard. Mark here tried to find out how he could locate Stearns to ask him if anything unusual had happened on his down trip, if Bob Ballard had acted sick or strange in any way."

"That was the last trip you know of?"

"If there was anything else, it will be on Ballard's record sheet."

"What record sheet?"

"The operators of that roof car keep a record sheet: who goes up, who cleared them, when they went up, and when they came down. At the end of his shift the operator turns in his sheet to the front desk. It's filed there.''

"You see them?''

"Not unless the operator or the man at the front desk thinks there's something I should see. I can't look at every bar or restaurant check or other written record all day long, Walter. I trusted people.''

"Can you get Ballard's file from the front desk for me?''

"It won't be there. He hadn't finished his tour of duty. He wouldn't have turned it in.''

"Where is it, then?''

"Probably in the car,'' Chambrun said.

"Not in the car,'' Hardy said. "We've been over it from top to bottom for prints.''

Chambrun glanced at the trash can, covered by a police tarpaulin. "On him,'' he said.

For the second time that afternoon I heard Hilda Harding's voice call my name from some distance away.

"Mark! Oh, Mark!''

She was standing in the doorway to the public corridor, accompanied by a uniformed cop. She came running toward me and, whether I liked it or not—and I liked it—she was in my arms, clinging to me.

"Oh, Mark! How awful! How terrible!''

"Lady thinks she saw something, heard something,'' the cop told Hardy. "She's Hilda Harding, a singer, filling a two-week engagement in the Blue La-

goon downstairs. She has a room on this floor—
1006."

Hardy smiled at me. "I guess you can verify that,
Mark," he said.

I guess, the way Hilda was hanging on to me, that
was a logical conclusion. I'd forgotten she had a room
on ten. The intimate time we'd spent together had been
in my apartment on two.

"I'm Lieutenant Hardy, in charge of this investigation, Miss Harding," the lieutenant said.

"Hardy—Harding," she said, blinking her bright
blue eyes at him. "We could almost be related!"

"I suppose."

"Except my real name isn't Harding," Hilda said.
"I invented it for the stage. I was born Wolenski,
Hilda Wolenski. My parents are Polish."

"You saw something, heard something, Miss Wolenski?"

"You better stick to the 'Harding,'" she said. "I
don't really answer to 'Wolenski' anymore. But I
thought, if I was under arrest, I had to tell you my
right name."

"You're not under arrest, Miss Harding. Just tell
me what it is you think you saw, or heard, or both."

Hilda looked toward the trash can. "He—he's in
that?" she asked.

"You don't have to look, Miss Harding. Now, if
you'd be good enough to..."

Her story was scattered, but in the end it led to something that mattered. She might never have gotten there if Hardy hadn't exhibited a patience I wouldn't have believed possible.

"I had a lunch date with Mark—which he forgot!" Hilda began. She wagged a finger at me and gave me a theatrical scowl. "First time anyone has stood me up for years! I caught up with him in the lobby about three o'clock, and for punishment I made him buy me a drink in the Trapeze. I had a rehearsal in the Blue Lagoon at a quarter to four. While I was scolding him, John Jericho, the artist, came in. I knew him by sight. He'd been in the audience at a night-club in Cairo where I was singing—oh, a year and a half ago. I know his paintings. It was exciting to meet him. Then, just as I was leaving, Mr. Chambrun came into the bar. Jericho joined him. I went on to my rehearsal with my piano boy, Billy Chard, in the Blue Lagoon. A little before five we broke, and I did some shopping in the boutique in the lobby. I came out of there loaded down with half a dozen small packages. It was just five o'clock. I know because I looked at the lobby clock— the big one over the front desk." She drew a deep breath, like a winded runner.

"So it was five o'clock," Hardy said.

"I went over to the bank of elevators and there wasn't a single one at the lobby level, except the private one that goes to the roof." She pointed toward the trash can. "He—he was standing in the open door."

"How do you know it was him?"

"It was the same young man I've seen every afternoon and early evening running that elevator," she said. "It was the regular operator, not a stranger. I asked him if he'd take me up to ten. He said he couldn't. 'I'm sorry, but this car is reserved for people who live on the roof and VIPs who visit them,' he told me. I told him I was a very important person, tried flirting with him a little. It didn't work, rules were rules. At that moment one of the regular elevators opened up and I had a way to get up to this floor, loaded down with my packages. I had some trouble getting my room key out of my purse—with all those packages, you see. But I managed. I went into my room, put down the packages, and started opening them to look at what I'd bought." She glanced at me. "A new negligee, stockings, some underthings. Suddenly I heard someone shouting out in the hall, like an argument—"

"You'd left your room door open," Chambrun said.

"I—I don't know. I don't remember," Hilda said.

"You must have left it open," Chambrun said. "Every room in this hotel is soundproof. You couldn't hear voices in the hall if the door was properly closed."

"With all those packages, I may have just tried to kick the door shut—and didn't make it," Hilda said.

"An argument, you said," Hardy prompted.

"More like a threat than an argument. One man was saying to the other that he'd 'better move, or I'll spread you out right here in the corridor.' I got to the door just in time to see him—" She pointed at the covered trash can. "You know, his uniform—and the door to the private elevator open. He'd just finished telling me, not ten minutes before, that he couldn't bring me to ten, but he'd brought someone else to ten. I called out to them to ask if there was something wrong. They both turned. My friend, the elevator man, looked white as death. I think he started to say something to me when the other man gave him a violent shove through the door to—to this place, and charged in after him."

"This other man?" Hardy asked.

"I didn't know him. I never saw him before."

"Can you describe him?"

Hilda shrugged. "He wasn't my type," she said. She looked at me and smiled. I got the message.

"Do your best to describe him," Hardy said. His patience was giving out and his voice had a sharper edge to it.

"Dark, suntanned, black hair slicked down," Hilda said. "He was wearing black glasses. I—"

Something like a jolt of electricity hit me. The man at the Trapeze Bar, the man Mitchell Prescott had asked about! I told Hardy and Chambrun I'd seen a man who fitted Hilda's description, that Mitchell Prescott had asked if I knew him.

"This guy rang some kind of a bell with Prescott," I said. "Thought he might have seen him in a mug shot somewhere. He got me to ask Eddie about him. He's been coming into the Trapeze the last few days, drinks alone, goes away."

"What time was it that you saw him?" Hardy asked.

"I wasn't watching time," I said. "But it was quite a bit after five. Mrs. Haven and Jericho had come into the Trapeze. I'd had a drink with Martha Madden. Then Mitch Prescott flagged me and asked me about this creep at the bar. I talked to Eddie about him. Then came a message from you that I was wanted in your penthouse. That, I know, was about a quarter to six."

"Was he there at five when Mrs. Haven and Jericho arrived?" Chambrun asked.

"I don't know. I had no reason to notice until Prescott asked me about him. That must have been after five-thirty."

"If he was there when they arrived at five and he was still there when Prescott asked you about him, he couldn't have been pushing Ballard around up here on ten at—would you say about ten after five, Miss Harding? It was five o'clock when you talked to Ballard in the lobby. You came up to your room, looked at your purchases from the boutique, heard the voices in the hall. Ten minutes? Fifteen at the most, would you say?"

"No more than that," Hilda said.

"So if this character was in the Trapeze at five, when Victoria and Jericho arrived, we can forget him," Chambrun said.

"But if he showed up there after he'd polished off Ballard?" Hardy asked.

"That makes for an interesting question," Chambrun said. "He knew he was seen by Miss Harding pushing Ballard out into this service area. Why would he risk going down to the Trapeze—having committed a murder—and stand there drinking? Miss Harding might show up there and his goose would be cooked. The one sensible thing on earth for him to do was to get out of the hotel on the double."

"Did you notice if this man with the black glasses was holding a gun on Ballard, Miss Harding?" Hardy asked.

"They were moving with their backs to me toward this place when I called out to them," Hilda said. "Ballard turned right around but this dark man just turned his head. I—couldn't see if he had a gun—I mean, I had no reason to look for one, you know."

Hardy turned to me. "Mark, you and Sergeant Cobb go down to the Trapeze. If this character is still there, I want him for questioning, and for Miss Harding to have a look at him. If he's gone, circulate. He could be somewhere else in the hotel—the grill, the dining room, the Spartan Bar. And if you see Mitch Prescott, tell him I want to talk to him. Maybe a murder will jog his memory about this guy."

TWO

SERGEANT JOE COBB was the uniformed cop who had brought Hilda Harding to the service area. He was right out of the book on what a good policeman should be: deadpan, humorless, and probably highly efficient or he wouldn't be working for Lieutenant Hardy.

Cobb and I went down to the mezzanine and around the balcony that circles the main lobby to the rear entrance of the Trapeze. It was just about seven o'clock and the bar was buzzing. The normal predinner crowd was there, and the news of a murder had somehow leaked and, I suspected, had gone through the Beaumont from top to bottom like a brushfire. I hadn't taken three steps into the place when I was surrounded by people with questions. The Beaumont's public relations genius was bound to have facts. I stalled them as best I could, promising that when there was something like a story to tell I would be available. My concern was for a dark, suntanned man wearing black glasses. He was no longer at the bar, or anywhere else in the Trapeze that I could see.

The bar was three deep in customers and Eddie, along with two assistants, was, as my father used to say, "busier than a one-armed paperhanger." I managed to get his attention and we went off into the little service pantry back of the bar.

"Jesus," he said to me, "Bob Ballard! One of the nicest guys we had!"

"Right now, Eddie, I'm interested in your one-drink friend with the black glasses," I said.

"Friend? Oh, that one you asked about before. He's been gone a little while."

"Hilda Harding has a room on the tenth floor," I told him. "She heard some people arguing out in the hall, went to look, and saw Bob with someone who could have been that guy. He pushed Bob into the service area where he was shot. That was maybe ten past five, quarter past. Do you remember when your friend first came into the bar?"

"He's not my friend," Eddie said. "I don't even know who he is."

"But you didn't notice when he came?"

Eddie was drying his hands on his white apron. "Around five o'clock Queen Victoria and that artist guy made their entrance. As soon as I saw her I started making her the drink she always wants—white wine, soda, a twist of lemon. The waiter came over and said the guy with the red beard wanted an Irish whiskey on the rocks. You know how it is. I was watching her and that damn little dog. That mutt always has something snotty to say to me when she walks past. She was all smiles, and a 'hello' to me, like always. Other people crowded around and then I saw we had that columnist bitch for a customer."

"Martha Madden?"

"Yeah. She has to be handled with kid gloves or there'll be some crack in her column about service in the Beaumont going downhill. Business always picks up when the queen arrives. I don't know how long it was, Mark—fifteen, twenty minutes, maybe even more—when I saw that queer with the black glasses standing at the bar. He hadn't signaled or anything; just waiting for me to notice him. Ordered his vodka and soda. Sometime after that you came over and asked about him. That sonofabitch can nurse one drink longer than anyone you ever saw. He didn't want to talk, so I let him alone. You left. I guess the boss had sent for you."

"To tell me about Ballard," I said.

"Damn! Such a good guy."

Sergeant Cobb got into the act. "So you don't know the exact time he came?"

"It was after the queen arrived, which would be five or a little after," Eddie said. "I didn't have any reason to clock him, Sergeant. I was busy."

"And you don't know exactly when he left?"

"Hell, I don't know exactly," Eddie said. "I knew he wouldn't be wanting a second drink. I left him alone. Place filling up. The boss turned up and took the queen and the artist guy away with him."

"Chambrun?"

"There isn't any other boss around here, Sergeant. He didn't speak to me or ask me anything about this guy with the black glasses."

"He didn't know about him then. But he knew about Ballard."

"Well, we got it on the grapevine a little after that and then this place really started to cook."

"And the man with the black glasses was gone?" Cobb asked.

Eddie shrugged. "He was there for a while—like the last few days—and then he was gone. I wish I could tell you what you want to know. He was here sometime after five, gone sometime after six. It's the best I can do."

"We may need you later," Cobb said. "A police artist may be trying to draw a picture of this man with the glasses."

"You know where Mitch Prescott went?" I asked Eddie. "I don't see him out front."

"He was here till a few minutes ago," Eddie said. "You might find him in the Grill. He usually has dinner there around seven o'clock when he's in town."

"Don't go home till I tell you," Cobb said to Eddie. "When we get a police artist here we'll want you to spend some time with him."

Cobb and I went down to the Grill, which is on the lobby level. It is a small, intimate room, designed to look like an old English chophouse, heavy beams, sporting prints, red-checked tablecloths. There are only about a dozen tables and you have to be in the good graces of Mr. Quiller, the captain, if you wanted a reservation there.

I spotted Mitch Prescott right away, sitting at a corner table, his bald head shining in the light from the chandelier over his table. I wondered if he ate with his pipe in his mouth, but I saw it resting beside his fork and knife as he contemplated some raw clams on the half shell. The pipe was always where he could reach it. He saw me at once and waved. Cobb and I went over to him.

"I hear you've got big trouble," Prescott said.

I introduced Sergeant Cobb. "The lieutenant in charge wants to talk to you," I said.

"Me? Why me?"

I told him about Hilda Harding and what she'd seen. He brought his fist down on the table so hard the silverware bounced.

"Damn! I've been torturing myself trying to remember where I've seen that character before," he said.

Chambrun and Lieutenant Hardy had moved out of the service area on ten with its gruesome trash can when Cobb and I returned with Mitch Prescott in tow. The housekeeper's little room on that floor had been turned into a temporary headquarters for the police.

"I take it our man wasn't there?" Hardy asked as we joined him and Chambrun.

"Gone, and no exact times of his coming and going from anyone," Cobb reported. "He arrived sometime after five and left sometime after six."

"You'd think the bartender would know," Hardy said.

"Why should he?" Chambrun asked in that strange, flat voice I hadn't heard until today. I knew just one word was spinning around in his head, "Ruysdale, Ruysdale, Ruysdale." Almost a whole day had gone by and nothing more than that first call from the kidnappers. He was with a friend, Hardy, and another friend, Mitch Prescott, and he didn't dare tell them what was eating away at him. "The bartender had no reason to keep tabs on time," he said.

"Was it after Mark asked questions about the man, asked them for me?" Prescott said.

"He doesn't remember times," Chambrun said, "and you don't remember what interested you in this man. Or has your memory improved?"

"It's the damndest thing," Prescott said. "I saw him standing there at the bar and I started to say to myself, 'That's'—and I couldn't come up with it. Had I seen a mug shot of him? Had I seen him in a police lineup somewhere? It just doesn't come to me! You understand, I see thousands of mug shots and go to endless police lineups. I don't think this man was someone I was looking for, just someone I saw in connection with something else."

"You don't deal with ordinary police cases, Mr. Prescott," Hardy said.

"Right. My concern is mainly with foreign visitors to this country," Prescott said. "Terrorists are everywhere, God help us. Anti-Jewish people, anti-Arab people, anti-American people, for God's sake. I look at the pictures of illegal aliens who are picked up, I look at them in police lineups and in detention centers. My particular job is to anticipate danger to people who come here to the United Nations, to Washington. Anyone with any kind of a record in terrorism or violence who shows up in this part of the world is brought to my attention. This man..."

"Yes?" Hardy said.

"I saw him somewhere. He obviously wasn't someone who concerned me at the time, or who he was and what he was suspected of would have stuck." He glanced at Chambrun. "You don't remember everyone who walks in and out the front door of your hotel, Pierre. Faces, faces, faces."

"I might surprise you," Chambrun said, "because anyone who comes into this hotel is my business. I happen not to have seen this man, but if I had, I'd remember when, and where, and why he interested me."

"In my case I have to learn to forget when someone doesn't concern me. But this one..." He made an almost comic gesture of pounding on his forehead with his fist. "It seems I've learned how to forget too well."

"I remember saying at the time that he looked like George Raft in an old Warner Brothers crime movie," I said. "Could it just be an old movie that you can't remember?"

Prescott gave me an odd look of surprise. "You know something, Mark? That just could be it! Every night of my life I go to bed, wound up like an alarm clock, can't sleep, turn on the TV set, and watch late movies. This man could be an actor, someone I saw playing a heavy. I don't really follow those late films; they just help me to forget the real world so I can doze off. It could have been a movie, and I unconsciously associated this actor with crime."

Chambrun turned away. "That was no late movie Miss Harding saw in the corridor out there," he said. "It was ten to fifteen minutes past five in the afternoon, only a moment or two before Bob Ballard was shot three times in the head, apparently by someone who looks just like your 'actor' in the Trapeze. It would be helpful if you'd go back to trying to remember where you saw this man and why the sight of him triggered your personal alarm system."

I'D NEVER SEEN a so-called police artist at work before. This guy, whose name I don't think I ever heard, was set up in Chambrun's plush office on the second floor. Prescott, Eddie, Hilda Harding, and I were brought there to help him. He looked almost like the cartoon concept of an artist: long hair, scraggly beard,

T-shirt, blue jeans, sneakers. I understand the police had come across him in some holdup situation in an East Side bar. He drew a picture for them of the gun-man who'd held up the owner, robbed the cash regis-ter, and taken off. After that the cops helped supplement his income by using him in cases like ours.

He began with my notion of George Raft in an old crime movie. The artist remembered Raft in a snap-brim hat. Eddie said no hat.

"Just slicked-down black hair, brushed straight back," Eddie said.

"Bigger, broader shouldered," Prescott suggested. "He must weigh about two hundred pounds."

We all agreed to that.

"I—I only had a glimpse of his face," Hilda said. "But his mouth in that moment—turned down at the corners—cruel."

The artist was quick, skillful, and in a few mo-ments he had what I thought was an exact picture of the man I'd seen in the Trapeze. The others agreed. Hardy had a picture he could circulate.

"If we catch up with him, I'll need you all again," the lieutenant said.

Hilda, after an inviting little smile to me, left, along with Eddie.

"You know someone in the State Department named Martin Stearns?" Chambrun asked Mitch Prescott.

"Sure," Prescott answered promptly. "Middle East expert."

"You have any idea where he would stay when he's in New York?" Chambrun asked.

Prescott held a lighter to his pipe. He smiled at Chambrun after he got it going. "I hate to say this to you, Pierre, but people do have favorite hotels that aren't the Beaumont. I don't know Stearns well enough to tell you whether his is the Plaza or the Waldorf."

Chambrun wasn't amused. "He may have been the last passenger Ballard brought down from the roof—if he isn't that man." He pointed to the artist's drawing of the Trapeze drinker.

"Hell, no," Prescott said. "Martin is smaller, slenderer, with prematurely white hair. Who was he visiting on the roof?"

"Guest in Penthouse Three," Chambrun said.

"Anyone I know?"

There was the briefest hesitation before Chambrun answered.

"Journalist named Larry Welch," he said.

"That figures," Prescott said. "Welch has been doing a series of stories on the troubles in Lebanon and other places over there. That's Martin Stearns's world. I can tell you there's someone in Washington who'll know where Stearns is every hour of every day of his life."

"It could help," Chambrun said.

"I could make the call for you, maybe save a step or two that way."

"I'd be grateful," Chambrun said. He gestured toward the phone on his desk. "Mark and I have things to do. I'll get back to you in a few minutes."

I had no idea what we had to do, but "mine not to reason why." I followed him out into the second-floor corridor and we headed toward the elevators.

"I've got to talk to Welch, try to reassure him that he's safe," Chambrun said. "If he doesn't already know what's happened to Bob Ballard, he will if he turns on his radio or his television set."

"How can you convince him he's safe?" I asked. "He isn't, is he?"

"Jericho," Chambrun said, not looking at me.

"You'll tell him Jericho is up there as a watchdog?"

"If I have to."

"But not the truth?"

He whirled around to face me, the hanging judge. "How can I, Mark? But if I have to, to persuade him to sit tight, I will."

Johnny Thacker was still running the roof car. One look at Chambrun and he knew enough not to ask him questions. I became his target.

"I understand your girl friend actually saw Bob's killer," he said to me. "Some fellow who's been hanging around the Trapeze for the last few days?"

"She saw a man with Bob who fits that guy's description," I told him. "You have any idea who he is, he stopped me in the lobby, three, four days ago, and asked me where the Trapeze was located. Jerry Dodd's just been asking me. I didn't happen to notice him again, but I understand he's been coming in every day."

Chambrun spoke. "Not today, though? You didn't see him come or go today?"

"No. I didn't see him come—and I've been on this car since about five-thirty. I wouldn't have seen him go."

"You haven't arranged for relief?" Chambrun asked.

"They finally located Lucky Lewis. He should be here any minute now. Mr. Dodd didn't want anybody on this car who hadn't operated the run before. Mike will take over for me if he gets here before Lucky." Mike Maggio is the night bell captain.

"Please don't leave the hotel without checking in with me," Chambrun said. "And I want every routine of running this car to be as it always is; no changes, no special things added. Tell Mike and Lucky that, whoever takes over for you. It's important, Johnny."

"It's your ball game, Mr. Chambrun," Johnny said. "But—"

"No buts," Chambrun said harshly.

It was almost dark when Chambrun and I crossed the roof to Penthouse 3. Daylight saving makes the twilight last until after eight o'clock in August. But lights had popped up all over the city, and you could see marine lights on the boats and tugs moving down the East River. Curtains were drawn across the windows of Penthouse 3, but we could see lights from inside around the edges. Chambrun rang the front doorbell and we waited. Nothing happened. Another ring, and nothing! Chambrun looked at me.

"Go back to the roof car and have Johnny call him on that special phone," he said. He was standing with his finger on the door button. We could hear the buzzing sound inside. "If he doesn't answer, call Jerry Dodd and have him bring the duplicate keys."

I turned to go, wondering how we'd blown it, when the door opened and there was Larry Welch, grinning at us. He was wearing a silk bathrobe, and he had a bath towel wrapped around his neck. His hair was damp, curly, uncombed.

"Sorry," Larry said. "I was under the shower when you buzzed."

Reading back over this, I realize that must have been the week I was obsessed with movie stars. George Raft drinking alone in the Trapeze, probably murdering the unfortunate Bob Ballard on ten, and here was a man who looked so much like Burt Reynolds you'd have to know them well to tell them apart.

"I was expecting you," Larry said, "but it's been a long day and I needed freshening up. Come in."

"Expecting us?" Chambrun said.

Larry's smile evaporated. "I heard the news on the radio—about your elevator operator."

The living room of Penthouse 3 is furnished in very modern stuff. It was occupied by so many different people from so many different countries that it had no nationality of its own. A big picture window at the far end of the room looked down over the river. The soft, flattering light, coming from wall and ceiling brackets, could have been planned by a skillful stage-lighting designer.

"There wasn't much detail in the news report," Larry said. "Just that he'd been found, shot to death, on one of the upper floors of the hotel." He glanced at me. "Did you know that when you were here earlier, Mark, asking about Martin Stearns?"

"I knew he was missing, had deserted the car. I didn't know then what had happened to him."

"Were you able to locate Stearns?"

"No," Chambrun said. "Now it's more important than ever. He may have been the last person to go down with our man from the roof."

"I'm sorry I can't help you to find him. They could tell you in Washington—at the State Department—where he's staying in town, if he is staying. I had the impression from him that he was heading back to Washington."

"He didn't mention any friends here in town?"

"Look, Chambrun, I don't know the man," Larry said. "He was someone I had to discuss my story with. He came to me because he's an expert on the background I'm involved with. It took him almost two and a half hours to go through the material I have. We didn't talk about anything except—what I had to show him."

"You say you didn't know him before today?" Chambrun's face was that gray rock again.

"We talked on the phone in Washington yesterday. I called him, told him what I wanted from him. He said he would meet me here at the Beaumont this afternoon."

"You weren't registered here at the Beaumont yesterday," Chambrun said.

Larry grinned. "But I was sure I would be. Your friend Claude Perrault said he had enough drag with you to insure it."

"You told us the material you have is very touchy," Chambrun said. "Something rather absurd, like it might be enough to start World War Three."

"That's not as absurd as it sounds," Larry said. "I needed Martin Stearns's judgment on how dangerous it would be for me to break my story."

"A man you didn't know?"

"A man whose knowledge of the people and the area involved made his opinion invaluable to me."

"You knew him by sight?"

Larry shook his head. "It just happens I'd never seen him until today. He works pretty much under cover, so he doesn't invite photographers to take his picture."

"So he just knocks on your door, says, 'I'm Martin Stearns,' and you show him material that could start a war?"

"I'm not a high school juvenile, Chambrun," Larry said. "Your man on the roof called me on the special phone. What's his name, Berger?"

"Dick Berger."

"He told me someone named Martin Stearns was waiting to be brought up. I asked Berger to check him out. That's part of the routine you told me was possible."

"Of course," Chambrun said impatiently.

"Well, Berger called me back. Told me the caller's ID checked out and I told him to bring Stearns up. When he arrived we chatted for a moment or two about our phone call of yesterday. He showed me credentials I guess he'd shown before—driver's license with a photograph, Social Security card, a passport. What more did I need?"

Chambrun reached in his pocket and brought out a folded sheet of paper. It was a copy of the artist's re-creation of the man in the Trapeze. "Is this Martin Stearns?" he asked.

Larry laughed. "Good God, no! Stearns is slim, about fifty, I'd guess, but with prematurely white hair. Rather elegant."

That seemed to fit Mitchell Prescott's description of the man.

"You're not telling me everything, are you, Chambrun?" Larry asked.

I held my breath.

"What you didn't hear on the radio," Chambrun said without a moment's hesitation, "is that a young woman, a guest of the hotel, registered in a room on the tenth floor, heard an argument in the corridor outside her room. That was about ten minutes or a quarter past five. She looked out into the corridor and saw our man Ballard and this fellow whose picture I just showed you. This dark man pushed Ballard into the service area. He must have shot him almost immediately."

"This woman heard the shots?"

"Soundproofing," Chambrun said. "Your man Stearns, leaving, may have been Ballard's last official trip. I thought he could have been the man in this picture."

"He isn't."

"But it's important for us to talk to him, Welch," Chambrun said. "The time is so close. If Ballard took your man Stearns down to the lobby, Stearns may have seen this man with the black glasses waiting to take the car up."

"I see."

"There's one other less pleasant possibility," Chambrun said. "It is that Stearns never made it down to the lobby."

That surprised Larry Welch as much as it did me.

"I don't understand," he said.

"Dick Berger brought your man Stearns up here a little after two, right?"

Larry nodded.

"Berger checked out your man, brought him up. There was a shift change at three o'clock, Ballard taking over for Berger. Ballard didn't have to check out your man when he took him down. He wouldn't have to check out another passenger who might be waiting for the car. It could be someone visiting me, or you, or Mrs. Haven, taken up earlier by Dick Berger. The security system checks people going up, not people going down!"

"You're suggesting this black-glasses guy was up here waiting to go down when Stearns left me?" Larry asked.

"And that Stearns may have been stopped at the tenth floor, too, only we haven't found him yet," Chambrun said.

"You mean?..."

"I'd feel better if we could locate him and get his story," Chambrun said.

"How could this black-glasses guy get up here in the first place?"

"He couldn't—theoretically—unless I cleared him, or Mrs. Haven cleared him, or you cleared him," Chambrun said.

"Well, I certainly didn't," Larry said.

"Nor I, nor Mrs. Haven," Chambrun said.

"Then how—?"

"No matter how secure the fence, how foolproof the lock, there is always a way," Chambrun said, and let it hang there.

Larry glanced at his wristwatch. "There must be someone on duty at the State Department who can tell us where Stearns stays in New York, or where he can be reached when he gets back to Washington—after working hours."

"I've got someone working on that for me right now," Chambrun said. "You know a man named Mitchell Prescott?"

"I've met him. Did a brief interview with him once," Larry said. "Big wheel in the CIA. How did he get into the act?"

"He called our attention to this man," Chambrun said, tapping the artist's drawing. "Saw him in the Trapeze Bar. Couldn't place him, but was certain he'd seen him somewhere—a mug shot, or a lineup of some kind. We were chewing that over when Hilda Harding—the lady I mentioned—identified this artist's drawing as someone she'd seen with Ballard on the tenth floor. Locating Stearns seemed important and Prescott said he knew someone in Washington who would know where Stearns was 'every hour of the day or night.' He may know now. Do you mind if I involve him with you?''

"Why not, if he can help?" Larry said.

Chambrun called his office. Prescott was still there, waiting for him. Prescott evidently came on the line, and Chambrun asked him if he'd mind coming up to Penthouse 3. "The guest up here is someone you know. Larry Welch. Oh? You have to be kidding! I'll arrange for the roof car to bring you up."

Chambrun put down the house phone and picked up the special phone to the roof car. "Chambrun speaking. Who is this? Good. Lucky, Mitchell Prescott will be ringing for you on the second floor. You may know him by sight; big fellow, bald head, always smoking a pipe. You do know him? Well, bring him up to Penthouse Three."

Chambrun put down the phone and turned back to us. I thought I'd never seen him look so hard and cold.

"Prescott knows where Stearns is," he said.

"That's great," Larry said.

"Not so great," Chambrun said. "You'd better fasten your seat belt, Mr. Welch. Martin Stearns is somewhere overseas, has been for ten days. He couldn't possibly have been here with you this afternoon."

Larry looked stunned. "But he was here! I checked him out! Passport and driver's license with photographs, a Social Security card. More than that, he had all the right answers for the questions I asked him. Prescott has to be wrong.''

''You better get some clothes on. After Prescott, there may be cops,'' Chambrun said.

The first thought I had when Larry Welch headed for his bedroom and clothes was that if Prescott and then cops started swarming over the roof, Betsy Ruysdale's kidnappers might decide Chambrun had broken their rules. If they had someone in the hotel watching, they'd have to know something was going on up here that wasn't ''regular routine.'' Whatever Chambrun was thinking, he kept it from me. He had moved over to the picture window at the far end of the room and was looking down at the river. He had to know that whatever he did in this situation might be putting Betsy Ruysdale's life on the line. The kidnappers had to know that Ballard had been murdered. It had been on the radio, probably television. They had somebody stationed in the hotel, they'd told Chambrun, and if that watcher wasn't deaf, the news was everywhere. They had to know there'd be a period of upheaval here on the roof. There was no way Chambrun could stop it. He had to hope, I thought, that if he could get things back to normal quickly, the kidnappers might decide he was playing ball with them. They probably knew, I told myself, who had murdered Ballard and why, and who the fake Martin Stearns was and what had become of him. I wondered if Chambrun was praying in his own special way.

Larry Welch had just come out of the bedroom, wearing a dark blue blazer, when the front doorbell sounded. I went to the door and let in Mitch Prescott, pipe gripped between his teeth, his eyes narrowed and colder than I remembered them being.

He nodded to me and said, "Hello, Larry."

Larry crossed and shook hands with him. "Long time no see, Mitch," he said.

"So what the hell is all this?" Prescott asked.

"It seems one of us has been had," Larry said. "You say Martin Stearns is out of the country and I say he was here for nearly three hours this afternoon."

Chambrun came over from the window. "How good is your source, Mitch?" he asked.

"How good is a ten-dollar gold piece?"

"Tell him your story, Welch, starting with yesterday," Chambrun said.

"Yesterday, around two in the afternoon, I called a guy in the State Department I know and asked if he could put me in touch with Martin Stearns." Larry gave Prescott his best Burt Reynolds smile. "I'm working on a story, Mitch. Stearns was the man who could tell me how hot it was and how dangerous it would be for me to break it."

"You know Stearns?" Prescott asked.

"Not personally, but I know his reputation. My story, which for the moment is off the record, is about someone Stearns knows very well. My friend at the

State Department reported back that Stearns wasn't available at the moment. I left a message for him with enough of a teaser in it to make certain he'd call me back when he was available.''

"You were here?" Prescott asked.

"Not yesterday." The bright smile brightened. "I was—somewhere else. Anyway, about five in the afternoon Stearns called me back. I told him I'd be here at the Beaumont today, and he said he'd be in New York himself and would come here to see me—and my material—around two o'clock. Around two-fifteen, two-thirty, the operator on the roof car called me and said Martin Stearns was waiting to see me."

"Stearns was in Tel Aviv yesterday, and he's somewhere in the Middle East today," Prescott said.

"The man on the roof car checked out his ID and brought him up," Larry said.

"A fake, a stand-in," Prescott said.

"I didn't know him by sight," Larry said, "so I checked him out too. There was a passport with photograph, a driver's license with photograph, a Social Security card. He was Stearns."

"What did he look like?"

"Like a bank president," Larry said. "Slim, well tailored, about fifty years old, I'd say; prematurely white hair."

"That checks, but it couldn't have been Stearns. I tell you, he's somewhere in the Middle East."

"He knew too much about my material for him to have been anyone but Stearns," Larry insisted.

Chambrun spoke for the first time. "There may be an answer to these contradictions," he said.

"A man can't be in two places, thousands of miles apart, at the same time," Prescott said.

"I think you should be able to guess better than most people how that could seem to be, Mitch," Chambrun said. "A big wheel in the CIA, you have to know how people work under cover. Martin Stearns is a very hush-hush diplomat. Right?"

Prescott nodded.

"So, let's say he's involved in something that requires him to stay out of sight. Officially, he's in the Middle East to anyone who tries to reach him. Larry's friend at the State Department told him Stearns 'wasn't available.' Larry leaves a message. It is important enough, intriguing enough, for Stearns to call him back. Stearns *is* available if you know how to reach him. He agrees to come here today. Now you, an important figure in the CIA, call Washington to find out where Stearns may be. Important as you are, you get the official cover-up for Stearns at the moment. He's in the Middle East and has been for ten days. Isn't it possible, Mitch, that if you get back to your people in Washington with your reason for needing to know where Stearns is, they may break his cover and tell you?"

"It has to be that way," Larry said. "The man who was here was too savvy to be anyone but Martin Stearns."

Prescott chewed down hard on his pipe stem. "My sources wouldn't have given me a cover story," he said. "And yet—it's just possible they didn't know it was a cover story. In Washington the right hand often doesn't know what the left hand is doing."

"Can you get back to your sources, turn the screws a little tighter, and see if you can get the truth about Stearns's whereabouts? If we could know for sure that Stearns left here in one piece, and is somewhere alive and well, it will keep the police from running down dead-end streets and keep this hotel from being turned upside down, unhappily concerned that there may have been a second violence."

"I can give it a try," Prescott said.

"Understand, Mitch, I don't need to know where Stearns is. I just need to know that he was here and that he left safely."

"He was here!" Larry Welch said stubbornly.

"I hope so, Larry," Prescott said. "I hope so, for Stearns's sake as well as yours. If someone stole his credentials, substituted photographs on his passport and his driver's license, then the chances are Stearns is in big trouble somewhere. I hope for your sake he was here, because if he wasn't, you've blown your so-secret story to someone who shouldn't have it. I'll do what I can to clear it up. Use your office phone again, Pierre?"

"Of course," Chambrun said.

We watched Prescott go out and across the roof to the elevator. I saw him standing outside the car door, an overhead light shining on his bald head. Off in what was now darkness I heard a short, sharp barking. Toto had spotted a stranger on the roof.

"I hope you're right about what may have happened, Chambrun," Larry Welch said. "Because if you aren't—well, Prescott is right, I will have blown my story."

"No World War Three?" Chambrun asked dryly.

"It depends on who saw my stuff," Larry said, and he was dead serious. "Understand, Chambrun, I don't blame you or your people for letting an impostor get up here to me—if that's what happened. I was taken in completely by his credentials, and I had twice the reason to make sure than your car operator had." He turned away toward the chromium-trimmed sideboard. "What I need now is a good slug of something. Drink, Chambrun? You, Mark?"

Chambrun shook his head, and, reluctantly, I had to play it his way. Larry opened the cabinet doors, revealing a well-stocked bar—provided by the management, incidentally. He poured himself a shot-glassful of bourbon, tossed it off, refilled the glass, and came back to us.

"Unless Prescott comes up with a quick and satisfactory answer," he said, "I'm going to have to leave here, Chambrun."

"Why?"

"If I showed my material to a fake, there are people who will want to see me down at the bottom of that river out there, wearing cement boots."

"You're not just being melodramatic, are you, Welch?" Chambrun asked in that strange, flat voice.

"It sounds like it, doesn't it? The research I've been doing for the last year will reveal treachery in very high places. It could topple governments and lead to a small war. In this day and age a small war could start *the* big one."

"What did the man you think was Martin Stearns advise you to do with your material?"

Welch held up his drink to the light and then swallowed it in one gulp. "He advised me to burn what I showed him and any copies of it I might have and forget about it. He knows I propose consulting one or two other experts, but he urged me not to do that, not to let anyone else see what I have. If what I've discovered leaks, not only is there the chance of a world upheaval, but I would almost certainly be inviting my own death."

"And you told him?"

Larry's smile was grim. "I told him I wanted a second opinion. My funeral, he told me. So you see, if he was Martin Stearns, I'm all right. If he wasn't, if he was someone impersonating Stearns, the wrong people know exactly what I've got and I may have a very short time left to live. They know where I am, and they obviously know how to get at me. I have to get out of here, as secretly as you can help me do it, and find myself some other place to hole up."

"I can't help you," Chambrun said.

Larry gave him a startled look. "A ride to the basement, a car with a trustworthy driver to take me—somewhere?"

"I can't let you go," Chambrun said.

"My dear fellow, with or without your help, I've got to get away from here. You can't stop me."

"I'm certainly going to try, Mr. Welch," Chambrun said. He turned to me and gestured toward the phone. "Ask Mrs. Haven and her guest if they'd mind coming over here, Mark."

I realized that the one way he could stop Larry short of locking him in Penthouse 3 and throwing away the key, was to tell him the truth.

"I haven't got time to socialize," I heard Larry say as I went to the phone.

"This is going to be about as unsocial as anything you've ever encountered," Chambrun said.

I got through to Penthouse 2. Mrs. Haven answered her phone and I told her Chambrun and I were next door and that he wanted her and Jericho to come over on the double.

"Your life may be in danger, Mr. Welch," Chambrun was saying as I rejoined him and Larry. "But there is also another life, very precious to me, hanging in the balance."

"I don't understand," Larry said.

"So listen!" Chambrun drew a deep breath. He was gambling for Betsy Ruysdale's life. "This morning my secretary, Betsy Ruysdale, who is also my very dear friend, didn't show up for work. I was in the process of trying to find out why she hadn't appeared when you arrived in my office. Shortly after Mark had settled you up here I had a phone call. Ruysdale had been kidnapped. The ransom for her release was not money. I was to handle your presence here in a certain way—or else."

"A certain way?" Larry asked. He looked stunned.

"I was to change no routines, I was to offer you no special protection. I was warned that every move I made was watched, and if I did anything unusual, Ruysdale would have had it."

"So you were prepared to trade my life for hers?" Larry asked very quietly.

"That's how it was put to me."

"So you let a fake Martin Stearns get to me."

"I had no way of knowing that, if that's what happened," Chambrun said. "Your visitor was checked out, regular routine. My man saw the ID that you saw and had no reason to question it. Neither did you. But

I didn't follow my instructions to the letter, Mr. Welch."

"Oh?"

"Have you ever heard of an artist named John Jericho?"

"Jericho? Of course. A brilliant artist, but more famous for being a sort of Lone Ranger against terrorism everyplace he touches down. The kind of storybook hero every ten-year-old boy dreams he can become."

"Well, he has touched down on this roof, Mr. Welch, and he's on his way here now." Chambrun stretched his fingers as though they felt stiff and numb. "I found myself facing a dilemma this morning that outdid anything I have ever come against in my life. I could do what Ruysdale's kidnappers ordered me to do and endanger your life; I could protect you, warn you, which was really my duty as the manager of this hotel and as a decent human being, and that way put Ruysdale's neck on the block. It—it was an impossible choice to make. I didn't make one, I compromised. I couldn't tell you what I've just told you because you would do just what you've threatened to do, pack up and leave. End of Ruysdale. Neither could I let you be a sitting duck. John Jericho is an old friend of mine and I asked him for help. We set up something—he is painting Mrs. Haven's portrait. Famous lady, famous artist. We made a big to-do about it, as though it had been planned for a long time. He's staying with her in Penthouse Two, ostensibly so he can catch her in the right moods, the right light. But he's here to protect you, to watch anyone who comes to the roof without an explanation.''

"Who knows the truth?" Larry asked.

"Mark, Jerry Dodd—my security chief—Victoria, and Jericho.''

Larry was silent for a moment. "From what I know about Jericho I couldn't feel safer if I were surrounded by an army. Prescott doesn't know?''

"No. If he did, the CIA might move in—end of the game.''

"My impulse," Larry said, "is to get away from here as far as I can as fast as I can. If the man I spent the afternoon with *wasn't* Martin Stearns, not only is my life in danger, but a dangerous conspiracy I am prepared to reveal can be covered up, buried, hidden, approached from some new angle. Maybe—just maybe—the safest thing I can do is stay put here, take whatever protection you can offer.''

"If Prescott finds out it *was* Stearns, then a large portion of your trouble drifts away," Chambrun said.

"Except I am still a target for your Miss Ruysdale's kidnappers.''

The front doorbell sounded and I crossed the room to let in Mrs. Haven, Jericho—and Toto.

"I've had to tell Mr. Welch the whole story,'' Chambrun said.

Jericho looked grim behind his flaming red beard. "Since you've done it, Pierre, there isn't any point in discussing the wisdom of it. But why?"

Mrs. Haven sat down in one of the apartment's modern armchairs, which surprised you by being comfortable, Toto on her lap. "I'm sure Pierre had a reason that makes sense," she said.

Larry Welch offered drinks, but only the lady took him up on it—white wine on the rocks with a twist of lemon. Chambrun laid out the facts for Jericho: the strong possibility that the Martin Stearns who had gotten to Larry was a fraud, the consequences to Larry Welch if he was.

"You're not willing to tell us what this 'conspiracy' you've unearthed is, Larry?" Jericho asked. He and Welch are the kind of people who get instantly on a first-name basis.

Larry shook his head slowly. "It isn't that I don't trust you all, John," he said. "But what I have is so hot that if I were to decide not to break the story, then anyone who knows what I know could be in real danger."

"And so will you," Jericho said, "unless you decide to spend the rest of your life on some deserted Pacific island."

"Unfortunately that may be true."

"This man who may or may not have been Stearns advised you to deep-six what you had and forget about it?"

"Yes."

"Would the real Stearns be likely to give you such advice?"

"Yes. That's why I planned to consult him and two other men who are due here tomorrow."

"But you would still be hung out to dry?"

"I didn't know, and Stearns, if he was the real Stearns, didn't know about Miss Ruysdale. I didn't know—and he didn't if he was real—that what you might call 'the enemy' knew what I was up to."

"What you were up to, where you were, what you planned. I understand Pierre installed you here at the request of a mutual friend."

"Yes. Claude Perrault, a Frenchman we both know well."

"He knew what you were cooking up?"

"Yes. In fact, he helped me gather the material I have."

"You trust him?"

"With my life," Larry said.

"I second that," Chambrun said.

"Until you told Chambrun, and Mark and Jerry Dodd and Victoria and I were given some hints, who else but this Perrault knew what you were working at?"

"Only Perrault knows," Larry said. "Chambrun and the rest of you don't know what it is—just that there is something. As I told you, Perrault really knows what I have, helped me dig it out, put it together."

"Could he have inadvertently let it slip to someone? Because someone knows. The kidnappers of Betsy Ruysdale know. Have you tried to contact this Perrault?"

"I have," Chambrun said. "He's out of touch at the moment. He works for the Paris Sûreté. He's on assignment, his wife doesn't know where."

"Look, Larry, either Perrault let it slip or you let it slip somehow," Jericho said. "If your Stearns was a fake, they know just how much trouble they're in. That adds up to your being a dead chicken!"

"I know," Larry said quietly.

"Let's try to pick a few nits," Jericho said. "Stearns, or the fake Stearns, came here to see you. Dick Berger, the man on the roof car, checked him out. You checked him out. He stayed here for three hours and then he left. Was there anything special about his leaving?"

Larry shrugged. "I called the roof car on that special phone, told the man on the other end—who was Ballard, I guess—that Martin Stearns was ready to leave, and would he please come up and get him."

"You said, 'Martin Stearns is leaving'? Or did you say, 'My guest is leaving'?"

Larry hesitated. "I think—I'm almost sure I said, 'Martin Stearns is leaving.' I had the impression the car operator kept a record of who came up, and would check out that person when he left." He glanced at Chambrun. "Am I wrong?"

"Each operator keeps a record sheet of comings and goings," Chambrun said.

"So what does Ballard's record sheet say?" Jericho asked.

"It's gone," Chambrun said. "He never got to turn it in, and it wasn't found in the car or on him. Ballard didn't take Stearns—if it was Stearns—up. Dick Berger did, checked his credentials, turned in his sheet when he went off at three o'clock. Not having taken Stearns up, Ballard wouldn't have recognized him when he brought him down."

Jericho's eyes were very bright. "Just a glimmer of light at the end of the tunnel," he said. "Maybe, by some chance, Ballard knew the real Stearns by sight. When he is told he is to come up here and take down Martin Stearns, he instantly spots the fake! He questions the man and he has to be silenced."

"But it was the dark man in the Trapeze who took care of Bob Ballard," I said. "Hilda Harding saw him."

"Has anyone ever suggested that we are dealing with only one villain?" Jericho said.

"It's a possibility," Chambrun said. "Ballard had a job in Washington before he came to work here. Stearns works out of Washington. He could have known the real Stearns by sight!"

"So, let's take that and run with it," Jericho said.

THREE

THAT WAS A figure of speech because nobody was going to run anywhere with the possible exception of me. Larry Welch, Jericho, and Victoria Haven were anchored to the Beaumont's penthouse level. Chambrun wouldn't leave the hotel or put himself out of reach of a phone there. Betsy Ruysdale's abductors might try to reach him with new demands. Jerry Dodd, the other member of our team, was anchored to Lieutenant Hardy's police investigation. The man in the Trapeze had to be found and questioned. Any number of people had seen him in the Trapeze for the last few days. Hilda Harding had seen him on the tenth floor shoving Bob Ballard into the area where he was murdered. How had he gotten up to ten? None of the elevators is automatic at that time of day. If he had been wandering around in the back service areas, he would almost certainly have been seen by some of the housekeeping staff or the maintenance people. Jerry Dodd's tedious task was to ask questions of dozens of people, some of whom had gone off duty since the critical time when the man with the black glasses must have been circulating.

I got the assignment to "run with it," Jericho's phrase. Did Bob Ballard's wife—widow, wasn't she?—know if Bob had ever mentioned Martin Stearns? When I left the hotel and took a taxi up to the Bronx, Mitchell Prescott had still not come up with anything definite. The normal workday was over in Washington. The people who man telephones and occupy offices in the evening and the early hours of the morning were not high enough to reveal anything that might be a department secret.

"Chambrun's theory could hold water," Prescott told me. I had stopped in the second-floor office on my way out and Prescott was still there, chewing on his pipe and waiting for someone to call him from Washington. "A man in Stearns's job could choose to be out of sight, out of touch with anyone but his immediate superiors. He *could* be covered by a story that he's out of town, overseas somewhere, and only one or two people would know the truth. I'm trying to find one of those people. So far, no luck. One of the things I did learn from one of the secretaries there is that the message Welch left asking Stearns to call is on his desk in his private office. If Stearns ever saw it, he just left it there. I'll bet my next paycheck he never got that message. Someone saw it, passed on the word, and a substitute for Stearns was set up and prepared to take his place. Anything new developed upstairs?"

I told him no and felt a little ridiculous doing it. Ruysdale's life was at stake, Larry Welch was in equal danger, and we had Prescott, with the CIA at his disposal, and Lieutenant Hardy, with the city police force at his, and we told them nothing. When it was too late we would have an army of professional crime fighters at our disposal.

I wasn't eager to face Anne Ballard and her two small children in their Bronx apartment. The police must already have been at her, and talking to a stranger would be the last thing in the world she'd want just now. Her husband had been brutally butchered only some three hours ago.

Anne Ballard was a pleasant surprise, if I can use the word *pleasant* in connection with someone who has obviously been ravaged by grief and shock. She answered the doorbell in her Bronx apartment, a pretty young woman except for tear-reddened brown eyes. She had reddish brown hair, worn shoulder length. She spoke before I could tell her who I was.

"If you are a reporter," she said, "I've been instructed by the police not to talk to anyone yet."

I told her who I was and that Chambrun had sent me. She stepped out into the hall, leaving the door almost closed behind her. "I've just gotten my two children off to bed, Mr. Haskell," she said. "I haven't told them yet what's happened. Bob wouldn't normally be home at this time—they didn't see him on a normal workday till breakfast. I just haven't figured out how to tell them yet."

"I understand," I said. "It's not something you're prepared for in advance."

"Oh God!" she said. She was fighting to hang onto her control. "Richard is five, Marilyn is three. They don't even know what death is! They found me crying. I told them I was sick, had a tummyache. They cry when they have tummyaches. It seemed natural to them. But in the morning—"

"I'm sorry, but I need to ask you—"

"I just wanted you to know," she said. "If one of them should pop out of bed, wanting something, I didn't want you to be the one to tell them—"

"I promise," I said.

"Please come in," she said.

The living room was a pleasant, homey, unstylish place. Comfortable furniture, a few pictures on the wall, one of a college football team on which Bob had played. A little orange light glowed on a Mr. Coffee machine on the sideboard.

"I can't offer you a drink," Anne said. "But if you'd care for some coffee? . . ." When I nodded she poured some into a china mug for me. "Cream? Sugar?"

"Just the way it comes," I said. The coffee tasted wonderfully refreshing. I realized I hadn't had anything but a drink in the Trapeze since breakfast. It was now about a quarter to nine in the evening. "I think you can understand why Mr. Chambrun isn't able to leave the hotel just now. But he asked me to bring you a message. You're not to worry about money, or making arrangements—any help you need."

"I haven't been able to think about what I'm going to need," she said. "But tell Mr. Chambrun I'm grateful for his offer."

"The police are still trying to check back on what happened," I said. "They have a lead to the man who killed Bob, an eyewitness—"

"Who? Who killed him and why?" She was suddenly a tigress.

"A girl who's singing in the nightclub in the hotel heard some kind of commotion in the hall outside her room. She looked out and saw Bob and this strange man in an argument. She called out to ask what was wrong and this strange man pushed Bob into the service area where, a few minutes later, he was shot."

"The police know who this man is?"

"They haven't caught up with him yet," I said. "He's been drinking in the Trapeze the last few afternoons, but no one seems to know who he is."

"Those children in there!" she waved toward the rear of the apartment. "They have no father now!"

"The last passenger we know of that Bob brought down from the roof on his car has dropped out of sight. We've been trying to find him to find out if Bob said anything to him, perhaps about the man our witness saw with Bob later. Has Bob ever mentioned someone named Martin Stearns to you."

She frowned, obviously finding it hard to focus on anything but her tragedy. "I don't think I ever heard that name," she said.

"I understand that Bob, before he came to work at the Beaumont, had a job in Washington, D.C. This Martin Stearns works out of Washington."

"It doesn't ring any kind of a bell, Mr. Haskell."

"What was Bob's job in Washington?" I asked.

"It was in a sort of State Department office building," she said.

I felt a little jolt of excitement. "Martin Stearns works for the State Department," I said.

"I suppose Bob might have known someone by that name," she said. "But unless there was something special about him, there wouldn't have been any reason for him to mention this Stearns to me. Bob came out of the army—Vietnam. He tried to find a job through friends and connections he'd made in the service. Someone recommended him for this job in Washington. It was kind of like a receptionist. He sat at a desk in the lobby of this building. There was no—no—what do you call it, name board? If someone wanted to call on someone in the building, they had to ask Bob. He would check on the phone to see if whoever the caller wanted to see was in and available. It bored him to death. He just sat at a desk calling people on the telephone. It was called a 'security' job, but it wasn't what Bob had dreamed of. He was in army intelligence in Vietnam. Then Johnny Thacker, who works for you at the Beaumont, got in touch and told Bob there might be something at the hotel for him. You know Johnny?"

"Of course."

"Bob and Johnny went to school and college together—Columbia. They played football together." She gestured toward the photograph on the wall. "We jumped at the chance. Richard was three years old and Marilyn was one. We'd be back here in New York, where we grew up and had family and friends. It meant we could find someone to stay with the kids if we wanted some free time together—a movie, or just out having a beer somewhere and listening to music. Johnny said once Mr. Chambrun got to like and trust you the job at the Beaumont could be forever." A little shudder shook her body. "Oh, God, Mr. Haskell!"

"It would have been forever, I'm sure," I said. "And know that it wasn't the hotel's laxity in any way that led to what's happened, Anne. Mr. Chambrun will stay with this just as long as it takes to make certain that the man who shot Bob is punished."

"Punishment I want," she said, "but it won't bring Bob back."

I couldn't tell her how complex the situation was back at the hotel but asked her if she could give me the address of the building where Bob had worked in Washington. She wrote it down for me on a slip of paper.

"Anything we can do to help you, Anne, with money, with arrangements for Bob's funeral, with the police, anything, call me at the hotel. I hope you won't feel you're dealing with a stranger when you ask for me," I said.

She touched my hand with fingers that were ice cold. "The thing I want most is to know what's happening!" she said. "It isn't as though Bob had been in an accident. Someone deliberately killed him."

"I promise," I said. "I'll let you know the moment there's any hard news."

I hated to leave her to sweat things out alone, but I had to get back with what I had. I had let myself be convinced of one thing. Bob Ballard, in his job in Washington, had been in a position to see all kinds of important people come and go at the State Department. He could very likely have known Martin Stearns by sight and would have detected a phony. He could also have recognized the dark man with the black glasses from the Trapeze, and remembered something about him that had so far eluded Mitch Prescott. That seemed the more likely, since the dark man appeared almost certainly to be the murderer.

Back at the hotel, I ran into a conference in Chambrun's office. Prescott and Lieutenant Hardy were there along with Jerry Dodd. I had to remind myself that this wasn't a gathering where Chambrun's real problem could be discussed. Chambrun, sitting behind his carved Florentine desk, looked to me as if he was just about at the end of his rope.

I told them what I'd learned from Anne Ballard, and handed them the address of the building where Bob Ballard had worked in Washington.

Prescott nodded. "That's the building where Martin Stearns has his headquarters," he said. "Ballard obviously knew the man he brought down from the roof was a fake."

"I got thinking on the way back that it could be something else," I said. "As we know from Hilda, it was the dark man from the Trapeze who was arguing with Bob on ten, shoved him into the service area, and probably shot him. He could have been the someone Bob recognized." I looked at Prescott. "That dark guy could have been from the Washington scene, couldn't he? That could be where Bob knew him, and where you must have seen him, Mitch, but can't remember."

"At least someone is thinking intelligently," Chambrun said.

Prescott ground down on his pipe stem. "Goddamn it, it just won't come to me."

"One thing I can tell you for sure," Jerry Dodd said. "Mr. Dark Glasses X isn't in the hotel. We've been over it, top to bottom. He just slipped away without anyone paying any particular attention."

Lieutenant Hardy was among the unhappy ones. "There are enough fingerprints in that service area and in that special roof car to keep us busy for a month. We have to lift them, see if we can find a set in each place that match, then fingerprint everyone we know was in both places legitimately to discover if there is a matching set that we can't write off. If we get lucky and find such a set, then we have to check the police files, the FBI files, army, what have you. Our man can have taken a slow boat to China—and arrived before we have a lead to him, if we get lucky enough to find a lead."

"Why complicate things, Walter?" Chambrun said. "We have two men we're trying to find. Prescott knows them both. Surely he will very shortly be able to tell us for certain whether the man who visited Welch was the real Martin Stearns or a fake. If he was real, we can forget about him." Chambrun's lips moved in a bitter little smile. "When that clears up maybe Prescott will find some way to jog his memory about Mr. X in the Trapeze."

Hardy suggested to Prescott that sometimes a uniform can confuse your memory of a man. "Maybe you saw him in an army uniform, a marine, air force, navy uniform. See him later in civilian clothes and he's familiar, but somehow the picture isn't right."

Prescott shook his head slowly.

"There are other uniforms," Chambrun said. "Doorman, bellboy, porter? . . ."

Prescott continued to shake his head. "I'm sorry, gentlemen, but it just won't come to the surface—yet."

"Thanks anyway for the 'yet,'" Hardy said.

Chambrun stood up. "If I don't get myself freshened up, I'm going to find myself walking in my sleep. Mark, will you and Jerry come up to my penthouse with me. We've got to discuss how to deal with the media. The hotel is crawling with reporters—papers, radio, television."

"I've given them the only facts we've got," Hardy said. "We have a murder. We're looking for a man whose picture I circulated. Prescott has suggested we leave Stearns out of all this until he's located."

"If Stearns is under cover," Prescott said, "we don't want reporters both here and abroad looking for him."

"When you say 'we,' do you mean the CIA?" Chambrun said.

"I mean State, the whole damned government," Prescott said.

"Well, the hotel must have something to say, too," Chambrun said. He marched across the office to the outer room, where another girl from the steno pool had taken over for Dolly Malone.

"Let the switchboard know that I'll be in my penthouse," Chambrun told her.

We went down the second-floor corridor to the roof-car door. Chambrun's three quick rings told the operator that it was the Man signaling. Lucky Lewis, the regular night man, was on the car.

"Any traffic?" Chambrun asked.

"Not since you came down, Mr. Chambrun."

"No one asking you for Mr. Welch in Penthouse Three?"

"No one, sir. Not for him, or you, or Mrs. Haven."

My stomach always turns over a little as the roof car zooms noiselessly up to the top. Jerry and I followed Chambrun into his living room. He went straight to his desk over near the French windows. He opened the deep right-hand drawer of the desk and brought out a little tape recording machine. I knew from experience that it was attached to his telephone so that he could tape any telephone calls he wanted to preserve.

"I had a call just before I went down to the office to check with Prescott," he said in the flat, dead voice he seemed to have acquired that morning—what seemed like years ago to me. "I want you to listen."

He pressed the "Play" button on the machine. The tape made a whirring sound, and then we heard a male voice.

"Pierre Chambrun?"

"Speaking." That was Chambrun.

"You've been treading on pretty thin ice over there, Chambrun. I warned you." A slightly British or Irish voice, as Chambrun had guessed.

Chambrun again: "One of your people murdered one of my people. There was no way I could block off the police."

"I know. Wrong man meets the wrong man at the wrong moment. But you've got to get things back to normal during the next twenty-four hours—or else."

"How is Miss Ruysdale?"

"I suppose I could say 'fine.' Fine but not happy. I'm going to let you talk to her in a moment. Let me tell you that the man the police want is miles away by now. There's no reason for the hotel not to go back to its normal routines."

"Put Miss Ruysdale on."

"Why not?"

There was a moment's silence and then Betsy Ruysdale spoke. There was no questioning her voice.

"Pierre?"

"Ruysdale! How are you, my dear?"

"Pierre, listen to me. You have to forget about me and do what you have to do."

There was the sound of an angry male voice in the background and Betsy Ruysdale was gone. The first voice came back.

"Not a very bright lady, your Miss Ruysdale, Chambrun," the man said. "She was supposed to tell you there was no doubt that we mean business. Perhaps we can scar her up a little so she'll always remember that we weren't kidding."

"If you harm her in any way—"

"Now, now, Mr. Chambrun, threats are a waste of time. If things are not back to normal routines by morning, Miss Ruysdale won't have to remember. She won't be alive to remember. This is the last time I'll be in touch with you."

"I warn you, if anything happens to Ruysdale—"

"Good-bye, Mr. Chambrun."

The tape machine started to make that whirring sound again. Chambrun touched the "Rewind" button. We sat silent for a moment. Chambrun's voice was a little unsteady when he spoke.

"How like her," he said. "'Forget about me and do what you have to do.' She knows I'm being asked to turn my hotel into a shooting gallery."

"I'll never forget that guy's voice," Jerry Dodd said. "If I ever hear it again, they're going to have to prepare a slab in the morgue."

Chambrun seemed not to hear. "The important thing is he didn't mention Jericho or Mrs. Haven. We may still be in the ball game, Jerry."

FOR MORE THAN twelve hours now I hadn't given much thought to my personal life. Remember, I was "in love forever." I'd seen Hilda, almost impersonally, around three in the afternoon when we'd had a drink in the Trapeze and she'd gone off to rehearse. We'd had no personal contact at all in the time she was reporting to Lieutenant Hardy what she'd seen on ten.

After listening to that frightening tape in Chambrun's penthouse I went back down to my own apartment on the second floor. My orders were to circulate, cool off the reporters, who would certainly be after me for information. My story was to be that the murder of Bob Ballard was something personal, something in his own life and past, in no way connected with the hotel. I knew that would send reporters churning around Anne Ballard and her two small children, and I regretted that, but we were playing a touchy game to protect two lives in real danger, Ruysdale's and Larry Welch's. I called Anne Ballard to tell her that she might be snowed under in the middle of the night by news people. She wasn't surprised. There'd already been reporters there before they'd had any lead from me. As I put down the phone in my apartment I saw a note lying beside it on my desk.

"Mark dear: Please, when you can, be in touch. I'm dying of curiosity. Love, love, love—Hilda."

Yes, I was in love forever, and I'd given Hilda a key to my apartment. She'd obviously been here, waiting for me till she had to do her thing in the Blue Lagoon.

My clothes felt as if they were sticking to me after this long day, so I shaved and showered, and put on fresh things from the inside out. It was normal for me to circulate about this time of night. I've been told I was imitating Marshall Dillon putting Dodge City to bed.

My first stop was to slip into the Blue Lagoon to tell Hilda I'd catch up with her after I'd done my duty with the reporters. Hilda was already into her eleven o'clock show, standing by the piano on stage, looking beautiful, with Billy Chard making soft magic on the keys behind her. She was singing an old folk song I'd cut my teeth on when I was a kid.

> When I was a young man I lived by myself
> And I worked at the weaver's trade.
> And the only only thing that I ever did wrong
> Was to woo a fair young maid.

> I wooed her in the summertime,
> And in the winter, too.
> And the only only thing that I ever did wrong
> Was to keep her from the foggy, foggy dew.

The audience loved it and clamored for more. She couldn't see me standing by Mr. Cardoza, the captain in the Blue Lagoon, at the back of the room. The stage lights were focused directly into her eyes, so that she couldn't see beyond the first ring of tables right by the stage.

"Tell the lady I'll be back," I said to Cardoza, who looks like an elegant Spanish nobleman. "When I get here, if you've got something hot that will go down easy—I haven't had anything to eat since breakfast."

"Leave it to me," Cardoza said. "Is there any news, Mark?"

"The only news is that there is no news," I said. I felt a little twinge of conscience every time I didn't tell the truth to someone I liked and trusted. "We haven't found the guy Hilda saw."

It would be hard to say whether the greatest amount of curiosity came from the reporters who had gathered at the hotel—along with an unlikely collection of rubberneckers who had wandered in off the street to view "the scene of the crime"—or from the hotel staff itself. Most of the people on duty now had come on after the tragedy on the tenth floor had taken place. Bob Ballard had been a much-liked member of what could be called a family. There was anger and a kind of grim determination to do something to help get justice for him. But do what? The police artist's drawing of the probable killer had been circulated, but almost no one but Eddie, his two assistants, and one or two waiters remembered seeing the man in the black glasses we were now calling "Mr. X." Apparently this man had not visited any of the other bars or restaurants in the hotel. No one outside the Trapeze remembered seeing him at all, except Johnny Thacker. Mr. X, a few days back, had asked him where the Trapeze was located. Apparently he had come in the last three or four days a little after five, gone to the Trapeze, ordered one vodka and tonic, nursed it for about an hour, standing at the bar, and drifted away. He had attracted no particular attention from anyone but Eddie. "One drink, no tip." The chance that he would turn up again, after having been identified by Hilda Harding, was zero.

Mike Maggio, the night bell captain, whose tour of duty was from seven in the evening till three in the

morning, had never been on the job during the hour
Mr. X had spent in the Trapeze each of the last few
days. Mike is a very sharp, shrewd, street-raised young
man who has a special eye for trouble and a photo-
graphic memory for faces. His tour is what might be
called a trouble time in the hotel, from the dinner hour
to the bar closings in the early morning. That is when
we get flooded by what we call "out-of-towners,"
people who aren't registered in the hotel, who patron-
ize the bars and restaurants, drink too much, and stay
up too late for the people who have to clean up after
them. Mike Maggio studied the artist's drawing of Mr.
X and shook his head.

"Never saw him," he told me. "Not recently, not
ever. But..."

"But what?"

"Could be a villain out of Dick Tracy comic strip,"
he said. "Almost like he was made up to look like a
bad guy."

"Mitch Prescott thinks he might have seen him in a
lineup, or in a mug shot," I said. "I suggested maybe
it was an actor he'd seen in a late movie."

"I don't get to see late movies," Mike said. "If I
did, I'd remember. I can tell you, for sure, this creep
hasn't been in the hotel during my tour for the last ten
years!"

A dozen or more police reporters, circulating in the
hotel, were no more help. These are men likely to
know by sight most criminals operating in the city.

None of them came up with anything when they saw the drawing of Mr. X. There were a few "it could bes," but nothing definite. I knew from Hardy that the police, trained to identify known criminals, had come up with nothing.

"Something about this smells," Mike Maggio said. "He comes here four days running, stands around for an hour in one of the busiest places in the hotel, noticeable because he talks to no one, meets no one, isn't a lush. One drink in an hour? It's almost as though he wanted to *be* noticed."

"And then gets caught as he's trying to kill a man?" I didn't buy it. Later on I could have kicked myself around the block for not remembering what a shrewd observer Mike Maggio is.

Perhaps, in retrospect, I can excuse myself for brushing off Maggio's notion. Something else had popped into my head. The roof car hadn't responded when someone else had called on Larry Welch. That was after Martin Stearns, real or fake, had left. There had been no roof car; Johnny Thacker had discovered it on ten and taken over so that Welch's caller could go up. I had gone from Chambrun's penthouse across the roof to Penthouse 3. It was to ask Welch about Stearns, and where we might locate him. He'd been occupied with someone and brushed me off rather quickly. Neither of us knew then that there had been a murder. But no one had ever mentioned that caller who was with him when I went there. Later it hadn't mattered. We knew, when Johnny Thacker took that caller up, that Bob Ballard was already dead, shot and shoved into a trash can. But it was a loose end.

Johnny Thacker had long gone, but I went to the front desk and asked Karl Nevers, the night clerk, to see Johnny's record sheet from the roof car. His first passenger, after retrieving the car from the tenth floor, was one Paul Dumont, cleared by Welch at 6:10, brought down again at 6:45. Short visit, probably unrelated but should be checked out.

I was on my way from the desk to the roof car when Mike Maggio flagged me down again. He was grinning.

"Lady in the Blue Lagoon has sent out a general alarm for you, Mark."

"Hilda?"

"You got some other chick in there who has to see you, come murder or high water?" Mike asked.

I glanced at my watch. Hilda would be going on for her last show in a half hour or so. I stopped at the entrance to the Blue Lagoon and asked Cardoza to let Hilda know I'd be there when her last turn was over.

"I have a beef stew keeping warm for you in a chafing dish," Cardoza told me. "French bread, a green salad."

"Oh brother!" I said. "I've got to see the boss. I'll be down as quick as I can."

Mr. Paul Dumont, Welch's last caller of the day, seemed unimportant when I got up to the roof. Mitchell Prescott was there with Chambrun when I walked into Penthouse 1. Chambrun looked almost out on his feet.

"No question anymore," Prescott told me. "The man who visited Welch wasn't Martin Stearns. Stearns is in Tel Aviv. I got him on the phone, talked to him personally. He never got a message from Welch. Of course he wasn't here."

"Does Welch know?"

"I was about to go across to tell him," Prescott said.

"Go with him, Mark," Chambrun said.

We hadn't gone ten feet toward Penthouse 3 when a dark shadow loomed up from behind Mrs. Haven's quarters to block our way. It was Jericho. A flashlight shone in our faces.

"We'd better arrange some kind of signal," the giant artist said. "Another time I might not bother to find out who it is." His light switched off.

I told him what the news was we were taking to Welch.

"I'll go with you, if you don't mind," Jericho said.

Larry Welch hadn't turned in. I guess it wasn't a night for sleeping for any of us. I thought he'd put a pretty good dent in the bottle of bourbon on the sideboard. He listened to Prescott with a look of disbelief on his face.

"If the man who came here with Martin Stearns's credentials was a fake, why did he just walk away and leave me with the material I have? He could have polished me off right here, taken the stuff I have, and walked out without anyone paying any attention to him."

"He knew you weren't going to break your story till you'd talked to some other people," Prescott said. "They have time to plan whatever it is they have in mind for you. You told this fake Stearns who it was you were going to consult, where they were coming from?"

Larry nodded. "Told him everything there is to know."

"Paul Dumont?" I asked. "You told this fake Stearns a Paul Dumont was coming to see you?"

"God help me, yes."

"Who is Paul Dumont?" Jericho asked.

"A courier from my friend Claude Perrault in Paris," Larry said. "He brought me some more material Claude had dug up in Europe. Believing Stearns was Stearns, I told him Dumont was bringing me evidence that would certainly help make my decision for me."

"And did he?" Prescott asked.

Larry's smile was grim. "I was sitting here when you arrived, thinking that if Stearns saw what Dumont brought, he would forget the advice he gave me about dropping the story. What Dumont brought me is a clincher."

"So you've answered your own question," Jericho said. "When you told this fake Stearns that more evidence was coming he had to have it—had to wait until you could receive it before he acted. Look, man, isn't it time you told us what this is all about? We need to know who to expect to be coming here after you.

Larry shook his head. "I can't. I need a green light from someone in authority before I can tell anything."

"Who has that authority?" Jericho asked.

"Who knows? Maybe only the secretary of state or the president himself! Understand something, Jericho. I'm sitting on a ticking bomb. It's going to explode no matter what anyone does. If I break my story, it will explode in one place; if I turn over what I have to someone in authority, it will explode but the damage may be different; if it falls into the hands of these bastards who are after it, it will explode somewhere else! There are two men coming here tomorrow whose judgment I will trust. I've got to sit tight until then."

"Who are these men who are coming?" Prescott asked.

"I can't tell you," Larry said.

"You're going to let them just walk into what may be waiting for them here?" Jericho asked. "You've told your enemies who's coming."

"The fake Stearns, you mean?"

"You say you told him who you were going to consult."

"If they knew Stearns was supposed to be coming, they'll know who else is supposed to be coming," Prescott said.

"They know now, for sure," Jericho said. "If you won't tell us, at least give them a chance to decide whether or not to come."

"Or arrange a different meeting place," Prescott said.

Larry glanced at me and I saw a question in his eyes. Was it all right to tell Prescott he couldn't move somewhere else because of the Betsy Ruysdale situation. I know Chambrun didn't want anyone in an official position to know. Larry made his own decision.

"I can't let these people who are coming know because they're traveling. I have no idea how to reach them," Larry said. "I can't relocate somewhere else because they won't know how to find me. I have to sit this out here, through tomorrow at least."

Prescott looked grim. "If this turns out to be something that will come my way in Washington, Larry, I'm not likely to forget that your hunger for a journalistic scoop kept you from taking help from me, from Chambrun, from Jericho."

"It isn't the story that matters," Larry said. "Not any longer. If the man who was here this afternoon wasn't Stearns, then the wrong people know exactly what I know and how I can prove it. I could never put a word down on paper and it would still be too dangerous for these people. They know I won't forget what I've discovered and it won't be safe for them to let me walk around with it stored away in my memory."

"So sooner or later you're a loser," Prescott said. "Give us a chance to help you."

"Like I told you, it's a ticking bomb," Larry said. "I told Stearns—or whoever he was—I needed advice on who to hand it to. They'll know where to toss it, where to explode it. Once that's done I've got a chance. It won't matter anymore whether I know or not. The whole world will know when the damned thing goes off."

Prescott shrugged. "It's your funeral," he said. "If you can't make your own decisions, you shouldn't be handling explosives. If you change your mind, I can provide you with the most sophisticated kind of help there is."

"I know," Larry said, "but I have to wait. The people who are coming to see me tomorrow will have the answer I need."

I have to say that I didn't know then whether Larry was inventing a gaudy melodrama to keep from telling Prescott that Betsy Ruysdale was under the gun somewhere, or whether what he told us was for real.

In any event, Chambrun's secret was intact for the moment.

Jericho gave Larry a kind of twisted smile. "You hear that little spaniel of Mrs. Haven's yipping, Larry, hide under the bed till you're sure it's a false alarm."

Jericho and Prescott and I started back across the roof, and, sure enough, Toto sounded a shrill warning.

"Nasty little beast," Jericho said cheerfully.

"You started your painting yet?" Prescott asked.

"In a sense, yes," Jericho said. "The first step in starting a painting is studying the subject. Paint and canvas will come tomorrow, when the light's right."

Prescott chuckled. "You shacked up with Queen Victoria?"

"About forty years too late for what you're suggesting." Jericho said. "But, yes, I am the lady's houseguest." He stopped outside the front door of Penthouse 2. "See you around."

Prescott and I rejoined Chambrun. The Man was sitting in a chair by his desk, head bent forward, his heavy eyelids closed. He looked up with a start as we came in.

"I must have dozed off," he said.

Prescott gave him the essence of what had happened in Penthouse 3. "If Welch isn't bulling us, you ought to provide him with extra protection if you don't want another murder in your hotel, Pierre."

"He hasn't asked for anything extra," Chambrun said, "and until he does I'm mainly concerned with the one murder I've got. Welch isn't going to be murdered while the place is swarming with cops and reporters."

I knew what he was thinking. Ruysdale!

MY JOB was to keep circulating while the night life was still active in the Beaumont. I might be of use somewhere, and I could act as a shield between Chambrun and the press, who were eager to get his version of things.

I was beginning to feel something like pain in my stomach, which I guessed was the result of slow starvation. I went down to the lobby, hoping Cardoza hadn't lost patience with me and was still keeping that beef stew hot! I knew I should have trusted him.

"Ready when you are," he told me, standing by the red velvet rope that blocked off new customers from an already overcrowded room. "Lady goes on again in about ten minutes."

"Maybe I'd better go back to her dressing room for a moment before I eat," I said.

"It's your stomach," Cardoza said.

I went around backstage to the dressing rooms and knocked on the door with the gold star on it. Hilda called out a "Come in!" She was sitting in front of her dressing table mirror, working on the finishing touches of her stage makeup.

"You brute!" she said to my reflection in the mirror.

I went over behind her and put my hands on her shoulders. I knew from experience that this wasn't a "hug-and-kiss" time. That would endanger the makeup so painstakingly applied.

"It's kind of a madhouse," I told her. "It's on radio and TV and half the nightcrawlers in the city are dropping by to see what there is to see."

She looked up at me, still in the mirror, and the fake eyelashes she wore onstage helped to make her eyes look wide as saucers. "I—I never thought I'd be scared," she said.

"Scared of what?" I asked her.

"Him," she said, "that creep! It's been hours and the police haven't caught up with him. Or have they?"

I shook my head.

"It's everywhere that I saw him just before he killed that poor guy, that I helped identify him for the cops. If he's some kind of a psycho, he may come back here, looking for me."

"The place is overrun with cops and security people," I said. "Just stay inside the hotel till they catch up with him and you couldn't be safer."

"When do you get off, Mark?" she asked.

"Closing time; probably around three o'clock."

"Could I—could I wait for you in your place?" she asked. "I—I'd feel better to know you were coming and would be there."

"Of course," I said. "But I have to warn you I may not be much of a lover this time around. I'm just about out on my feet."

She turned around and looked directly at me. "Sometimes you just need to be close to someone you care about," she said. She reached up and touched my cheek with her fingers. "I care for you, Mr. Haskell."

"That's made my day," I said. I bent down to kiss her but she leaned away.

"You'll spoil my face," she said. "I've got to get moving now, Mark."

"I'll see you as soon as they'll let me up," I said.

Cardoza had saved me a little corner table out front. I could take a lot of space describing his beef stew, but it's really not part of the story. It's enough to say that it made a new man of me. While I was eating it the lights dimmed and Billy Chard came out onstage to a ripple of applause, and began doing some ups and downs on the piano. Then Hilda came out and they tore the place apart for her. She leaned against the piano and began singing Jerome Kern's great old song from *Show Boat*.

> He's just my Bill,
> An ordinary man...

Wherever Helen Morgan is—here or in the hereafter—she would have to be jealous if she were listening.

I finished my stew and slipped out quietly while Hilda was still doing her thing. The lobby had a strange feeling of being out of order. Cops and reporters, who didn't normally belong, seemed to be everywhere. I couldn't take three steps in any direction without someone stopping me to ask if there was anything new.

A little after two o'clock I saw people flooding out of the Blue Lagoon and I knew that morning's playtime was coming to an end. I checked out with Mike Maggio, told him I'd be in my apartment if there was any kind of crisis.

He gave me what might be classified as a leer. "I don't imagine you'll be up to any kind of crisis but your own," he said. "The lady went up to your place not long ago."

"She wearing a sign?" I asked.

"We're just not letting people wander around tonight without asking them where and why," Mike said. "She told me where—but not why!"

Mike's comedy at that hour of the morning didn't enchant me. I took an elevator up to two and walked along the corridor to the door of my apartment. The south end of the second floor includes Chambrun's suite of offices, the accounting department—closed for the night—my place, and my office at the east end of the corridor—also closed for the night. I unlocked the door to my place and went in. There were a couple of lights burning in the living room, but no Hilda. I walked over to the bedroom door, and in the light from the living room I saw her stretched out on my bed.

"Better late than never," I said.

She didn't answer, I walked over and sat down on the edge of the bed beside her. "Hey, wake up," I said.

She didn't respond and I reached out and turned on the light on the bedside table. I think I came as close to screaming as I have ever come in my life. Her tongue was sticking out of her mouth, swollen and dark with blood. Her eyes seemed to be popping out of her head, staring at the ceiling. There were cruel marks and scratches on her throat.

Hilda had been strangled to death.

Part Three

ONE

IT'S HARD TO describe how I felt in that moment of horror. I am not totally unaccustomed to violence. It has happened in Chambrun's world over the years I've worked for him, just as it happens in the outside world multiplied by thousands. Violent things, some of a criminal nature, some by way of accidents, have happened to people I know. Less than ten hours ago Bob Ballard, someone I knew and liked through my job, had been brutally murdered. But this was something else! I had held this once lovely girl in my arms, laughed and joked with her, and made exciting love with her.

I think I should say here—so that you won't be feeling sorry for me in the wrong way—that when I say I was "in love forever" with Hilda it was a joke of sorts. I knew that when her engagement at the Blue Lagoon was ended and she moved on to her next job in some other city it would be over. I'm not a guy who is partial to the one-night stand. I like a period of time with someone, a few days, a few weeks, a few months if it pans out. Someday I think it will be "forever" with someone. With Hilda? It might have been, it could have been. It wasn't to be.

I reached for the telephone on the bedside table and asked to be connected with Jerry Dodd. He'd turned in after hours on the go and he answered, sleepy and a little angry at being disturbed.

"I'm in my apartment," I told him. "Hilda Harding is here. She's been strangled, Jerry. She's dead."

Jerry has a cop's mind. "Don't touch anything," he said.

"Police?" I said.

"I'll handle it," Jerry said. "You want me to call Chambrun?"

"If you will. I'm just not—"

"I understand. Stay put. Don't touch anything!"

I didn't follow his instructions to the letter. I went into the bathroom and took a clean towel off the rack there. I contemplated the possibility of throwing up, and then I realized that the turmoil I felt in my gut was a fierce, growing anger, not nausea. I went back into the bedroom and covered that ghastly face with a hand towel. I was telling myself that Hilda wouldn't want anyone to see her that way. It was absurd, of course, because the police would look at her, and the medical examiner's boys, and the police photographers.

I went out into the living room. A couple of things I was going to touch in spite of Jerry's warning. They were a glass and a bottle of Jack Daniel's. I poured a good four ounces into a glass and drank it in one long gulp. It went down like water. I guess I was beyond feeling anything.

Then Jerry was ringing my doorbell. He looked tense, like a tiger about to attack. "Where is she?"

"In the bedroom."

I followed him as he streaked across the living room. He stood in the doorway. "You found her like that, towel over her face?"

"I—I couldn't stand looking at her, or having anyone else see her the way she is."

"I told you not to touch anything!"

"I didn't touch anything but a clean towel—and a bottle and a glass on the sideboard in here."

He went over, lifted the towel, and stood looking down at—what was there.

"Jesus!" I heard him whisper. He turned back to me. "Hardy's on his way, you found her like this? What was she doing here?"

"Waiting for me," I said.

"You brought her up here?"

"She—she had a key."

"Oh, brother, you don't know when she came, then?"

"I saw her in the Lagoon just before she went on for her last show," I said. "She was scared. She asked if she could come up here and wait for me when I got off the hook."

"Scared of what?"

"The guy she identified for Hardy, Ballard's killer."

"How did he get in? The door wasn't forced, was it left unlocked?"

It was hard to go back over it. "It wasn't forced. It was locked when I came up here. I opened it with my own key."

"Where is her key?"

"I don't know. In her purse, I suppose. You told me not to touch anything."

He started to pick up her bag, which was lying on the floor beside the bed, and changed his mind. "I'll leave that for Hardy," he said. "God, Mark, I'm sorry. I know how hard it is for you to take. But two in less than twelve hours!"

"Chambrun?" I asked.

"He hoped you'd understand why he won't come running," Jerry said. "He might be hearing from—someone."

"He thinks it may be connected with what's happened to Ruysdale?"

"You said it yourself," Jerry said. "That man identified by your girl as Ballard's killer. 'Wrong man at the wrong time in the wrong place.' Isn't that what Ruysdale's kidnapper said to the boss on the phone?" He looked back at Hilda's body. "When did you give her the key?"

"A week ago, I guess. She and I—"

"I read you," Jerry said. "You had a thing going, right?"

"You could say—"

"I don't give a damn what you do with your private life, Mark," Jerry said. "But what you do with your keys may be important. Who else has one?"

"No one."

"Not some chick who resented the Harding girl moving into her place?"

"The only other spare key is in the key locker back of the front office." The key locker contains duplicate keys to everything that has a lock on it in the hotel. Not just anyone could walk in there and take a key off a hook. There was someone at the desk, just in front of the key-locker door, round the clock.

"The reason I'm making such a point of this, Mark—if no one else has a key and the door wasn't forced, then Miss Harding brought someone up here with her, or she let someone in after she got here."

"People followed her everywhere trying to get autographs," I said. "She was generous to kids wanting her to sign something."

Jerry's voice was grim. "You think a kid did that? She must have put up a fight."

I pointed out to him that there wasn't any sign of a fight. She just lay there on top of the bed, fully clothed, dead. No mess-up anywhere else in the room. "She could have been slugged from behind, strangled when she was unconscious," I said.

"Could be. We'll have to wait for the medical examiner to tell us," Jerry said. "Who knew she was coming up here?"

"I guess quite a few people guessed at it, joked about it," I said. "What you do in this hotel is like living in a fishbowl. And Hilda and I didn't try to hide the fact that we had something going."

"I mean tonight—who knew?" Jerry said.

"Mike Maggio, for one," I said. "He told me Hilda was up here. They weren't letting people wander around tonight, he told me. Hilda told him she was headed for my place. He's off duty now, I suppose."

"Not tonight," Jerry said. "I asked him to stay around in case we needed extra help." He took a handkerchief out of his pocket, used it to pick up the bedside phone I'd used to call him, and asked the switchboard to locate Mike and send him up to my place.

I had an idea while he was talking and I passed it on to him when he put down the phone. "It just occurred to me, Jerry, there could have been someone in here when Hilda let herself in. She saw him, started to go for help—"

"You say no one else has a key."

"Some of the hotel thieves we have around are magicians with locks," I said.

"The lock can tell us that when Hardy gets here to look at it," Jerry said. "No matter how good you are, you can't open a lock with a burglar tool without leaving fresh scratches. We'll see."

When you don't want a policeman, there's always one right there. When you do, they seem to take forever. Mike Maggio turned up before Hardy and his people arrived. He hadn't been told on the phone why he was wanted. He had a kind of mischievous smile on his street-smart face when Jerry let him into my living room. I guess he had some kind of wisecrack ready, but a look at Jerry and me must have told him he hadn't been invited to a party.

"What's wrong?" he asked.

Jerry pointed to the bedroom door and Mike walked over and took a look. "Oh, boy!" I heard him say. He turned back to us. "Oh, boy, Mark, you found her that way?"

I nodded.

"Sonofabitch!" Mike said.

"Who got up here tonight, Mike?" Jerry asked.

That may sound to you like an absurd question in a hotel where hundreds of people are circulating in the evening pleasure hours. I have to go back to geography again. The south and north ends of the building are the narrow ends. The lobby goes up three floors in open space, surrounded by the mezzanine gallery, where anyone can sit and look down at the people moving about, with the Trapeze Bar on the west side, beauty parlors and a barber shop on the east side. The second floor is really just the narrow north and south ends. My end, the south, as I have said, is just Chambrun's suite of offices, the accounting department, my apartment, and my office.

"You know, Jerry, it isn't because anything special happened here today," Mike said. "Every night, after the close of the business day—seven o'clock, when I come in—the south bank of elevators don't stop at two, unless it's Mark—who, of course, can come and go at anytime because he lives here—or the boss or Miss Ruysdale wanting to go to his office. And, of course, anyone we know has legitimate business with those people. Or someone, like Miss Harding, whom I knew had—well, would be welcomed by Mark. There's the one stairway, but that we watch. Particularly tonight we watched. I can tell you that no one who didn't belong went up to the second floor on my shift except Miss Harding, and I figured—well, that she did belong there."

"You spoke to her?" Jerry asked.

"Yeah, sure. She asked me if I'd tell the elevator operator to let her off at two. 'I'm going to wait for Mark up there,' she told me. I kind of laughed and said, 'Out in the hall?' She said, 'I have a key.' I said something silly like 'Naughty, naughty!' She kind of grinned at me and said, 'But what fun!' That was it. People can get to the second floor from up above, Jerry, by using the fire stairs."

"I know. No special reason for us to guard this floor," Jerry said. "Hotel thieves are after rich guests with cash and jewelry."

And then the troops arrived, headed by Lieutenant Hardy. They all went into the bedroom and I could hear exclamations of surprise and anger from them. Hardy reappeared, his broad, pleasant face hard.

"You found her that way, Mark?"

"Yes."

"This place isn't going to be very livable for the next few hours," the lieutenant said. "We're going to have to dust it from one end to the other for prints. You touch anything since you came in?"

I told him the telephone and light by the bed where Hilda lay, the towel I'd brought from the bathroom, the glass and bottle on the sideboard. "But I was here earlier in the evening, Walter, shaved, showered, changed my clothes. Touched a hundred things, I suppose."

"We'll need your prints so we can eliminate," Hardy said. "Sergeant Cobb will take them. Can we talk in Chambrun's office?"

"If he says so."

"He'll say so," Hardy said. "Why isn't he here?"

"Someone has to steer the ship," Jerry Dodd said quickly. He knew why Chambrun wasn't here. Ruysdale!

COBB TOOK my prints, smearing me with ink I couldn't seem to wash off. The bedroom in my place was no-man's-land, except for fingerprint geniuses, photographers, and men from the medical examiner's office. I went down the hall to Chambrun's offices, switched on lights, and went into the Man's private sanctum. The first thing I noticed was a stack of knocked-out pipe ashes in the brass tray on the desk. Prescott had been using the phone here off and on. I was reminded that Ruysdale wasn't with us. That ashtray would never have been left unemptied on Chambrun's desk.

I called the Man's penthouse and got him on the first ring.

"Oh, it's you, Mark," he said in that flat voice I hadn't gotten used to hearing from him.

"Anything on your end?" I asked.

"No." It was flat, cold, and hard. He was wearing awfully thin, I thought. Then he was himself. "I'm so very sorry for you, Mark."

"It's pretty gruesome," I said. "Hardy's in charge. I'm in your office, waiting to play questions-and-answers with him."

"You, personally, have no thoughts on it?"

"I haven't really been up to thinking much," I said. "Finding her—that way..."

"Anything in her personal life, Mark, that you know about?"

"Nothing. We—we hadn't gotten to talking about that sort of thing. All that mattered to us was 'right now.'"

"Keep me posted when you can," Chambrun said. I thought he made a kind of choking sound. "Pretty soon, Mark, I've got to stop playing it their way and play it mine."

"Meaning?"

"Get through with Hardy and we'll talk," he said.

I've said Lieutenant Hardy looked like a professional football linebacker. He looked now like one who had just stopped up the wrong hole and someone had run for a touchdown.

"There's no place to get started back there," he said, when he joined me in Chambrun's office. "Jerry Dodd and Maggio have caught me up on all the things that don't help us. We've got to get to the girl, Mark."

"I can't help much," I said.

"Let's get one thing straight between us," Hardy said. "I think of you as a friend—quite a number of years. This time, though, you're an actor in this script. I've got to treat you like a cop. This is an official interrogation." He gestured toward the uniformed policeman who'd come with him. "Moncrief will be taking it down."

Moncrief, the cop, had put a stenotype machine down on Chambrun's desk and taken his place behind it.

"So this is for the record," Hardy said. "The girl's name is Hilda Harding?"

"That's a stage name, professional name," I said. "Her real last name is Wolenski. Polish."

"You know anything about her family?"

"Look, Walter, before we go any further there's someone who can tell you a lot more about her than I can. Young fellow who plays the piano for her named

Billy Chard. Been with her several years, I understand. He's registered here in the hotel."

Hardy made a signal to Moncrief, who picked up the phone and started to track down Chard.

"He knows her better than you do," Hardy said, "but she had a key to your apartment, negligee hanging in your closet. How much better could anyone know her?"

"Walter, you're married, got three grown kids. You wouldn't understand."

"That a pretty girl is tempting?"

"You wouldn't let yourself be tempted," I said.

"How long had you known this girl?"

"Two weeks. She started her engagement in the Blue Lagoon two weeks ago."

"Not before that?"

"No. Oh, I'd heard some of her records, but I'd never seen her or met her till the night she opened here."

"And she moved right in with you?"

"That very first night," I said. I knew that would shock him. "I went into the Lagoon to hear her sing. She was marvelous. I bought her a drink when she was done and—and we wound up in my apartment."

"Just like that?"

"Just like that. Look, Walter, I'm not married, I don't have any commitments to anyone. As far as I know, neither did Hilda. Our wires touched, and—and we took off."

"And she's been shacked up with you for two weeks?"

"That's a vulgar phrase, Walter," I said, grinning at him. "We've been having marvelous sex together for two weeks."

"Plans for the future?"

"She had another week to go here. Then she was off to Vegas, I think. That's as far as we planned."

Hardy tugged at an ear. "Let's start over," he said. "You're with her every night for two weeks. You must have talked about something. Her family? Boyfriends she'd had? Enemies she'd made?"

"You'd be surprised how little talking of that kind we did. We'd get together about three in the morning, when she'd done her last show and I could finally stop circulating. I had to be up at eight to meet Chambrun here at nine. We did damn little talking, Walter."

"Dodd says she asked you if she could come up to your place tonight, that she was scared."

"She knew it wasn't a normal night," I said. "I would be tied up, wouldn't expect her. But she was nervous about the man you haven't caught. If he was some kind of psycho, he might come back here, looking to get at her for having identified him for you. She didn't feel safe up on the tenth floor. I don't blame her, do you?"

"Did she say anything more about our Mr. X? Did she remember him from someplace else?"

"She didn't say anything like that to me. I've been on the run, as you know. I saw her for two or three minutes before she went on for her last show. She just said she was scared. That didn't seem unnatural to me."

Hardy made a little gesture to Moncrief, the cop on the stenotype, to let him know that what was coming next was off the record.

"The interrogations in a murder case are open to many eyes," he said, "particularly the district attorney and his smart-assed boys. A young man's current girl friend is found strangled to death in his apartment, he is certainly a primary suspect. I've got to ask you questions that I would ask a stranger in the same situation. I don't think you killed the girl, Mark, but officially I have to handle you just as I would someone I never laid eyes on before."

"You could disqualify yourself," I said, trying to make it sound funny.

He gave me an unexpectedly hard look. "I wouldn't advise you to suggest that," he said. "You'd find yourself under some very bright lights answering some very sticky questions."

"Sorry, Walter," I said. "I haven't had anything to laugh at for hours and hours. I was just trying to be funny."

He signaled to Moncrief and I knew we were back on the record again. "You say you'd finished your tour of duty, come up to your apartment, found the

Harding girl lying on your bed, fully clothed, strangled.''

"Yes.''

"What time was that?''

"I don't punch a clock, Walter. I do what I have to
do and I stay with it till it gets done. I'd say it was a
little before three, because Mike Maggio was still on
duty. He goes off at three. He spoke to me on my way
up, told me Hilda was in my apartment.''

"You been drinking?''

"'Drinking,' no,'' I said. "Had I had a few drinks?
Yes. Starting at lunchtime and until I turn in about
three in the morning I have half a dozen drinks every
day of my life.''

"What was your special duty tonight?''

"My special duty was handling an army of reporters from the papers, the radio, and TV. We've set up
a private room for them at the north end of the lobby.
I was to keep them out of Chambrun's hair—and
yours. That went with my regular duties, which are to
circulate in the Blue Lagoon, the Trapeze, the Spartan Bar, any special events in the ballroom—nothing
there tonight.''

"So you're pretty much on the move all evening?''

"Yes.''

"I understand the south end of the second floor is
shut off after seven o'clock in the evening. But you
could come and go without anyone paying any particular attention.''

"True."

"What time do you think the girl went up to your apartment?"

"I don't know, but Mike Maggio might be able to tell you. He talked to her. She asked him to tell the elevator operator to let her off at two. I could guess."

"So guess."

"Her last turn in the Lagoon is at one o'clock. I saw her start. I was eating something out front. I left before she finished. But her turn lasted for about forty-five minutes."

"A quarter to two?"

"Just about, unless the audience wouldn't let her go on the dot. Then she went back to her dressing room and changed out of her stage clothes."

"How do you know that?"

"Because she wasn't wearing a costume dress when I found her, and she'd taken off her stage makeup."

"How long would it take her to take off her makeup and change clothes?"

"Ten, fifteen, twenty minutes, depending on how much of a hurry she was in."

"So we can assume she got up to your apartment at two or a little after?"

"I'd say so, but again, Mike Maggio can probably be more exact."

"So there was something like an hour after she got up to your place and the time you went up there and found her?"

"About that, I'd guess."

"But you could have gone up there in that hour, unnoticed, killed her, gone back downstairs, and made sure you were noticed when you went back up at three."

"Oh, for Christ's sake, Walter!" I said.

"You could have."

"Why would I want to kill her, for God's sake!"

"You tell me. Lover's quarrel; you'd both been drinking more than you'll admit; she had something on you."

"I'd been robbing the hotel? Come off it, friend!"

"I'm not your friend at the moment, Haskell." That was for the record, I supposed.

"Look," I said, "I wasn't in hiding for that hour. Nor did I have any reason to provide myself with an alibi. If I were to sit down and think, I might be able to tell you everyone I talked with, spent any time with. It should cover me."

"You do just that," Hardy said. He signaled to Moncrief that the interrogation was over for the moment. The palms of my hands felt a little damp, even though my conscience was in perfect shape. There's a special kind of toughness about a cop at work, even though he's your friend.

The door at the far end of the office opened and Jerry Dodd came in, bringing Billy Chard with him. Billy is a handsome young guy: wavy brown hair worn longish, wide brown eyes that were red now from

weeping. I'd never seen him wearing anything but the
beautifully tailored dinner jacket that was his uniform for Hilda's performances. I'd never had any
conversation with him except to tell him how great I
thought he was on the keyboard. I assumed from a
couple of things Hilda had let drop that he was gay.
He wasn't his elegant self now. He had on a brown
turtleneck sweater, tan slacks, and a pair of brown
loafers. He was carrying a crumpled handkerchief in
one hand, which he kept raising to his eyes and then
lowering to his mouth. I was the only person he knew
in the room, so I guess he took aim at me.

"You bastard!" he said.

"He didn't know, of course, when I woke him,"
Jerry Dodd said.

"Sit down, Mr. Chard," Hardy said, and when
Billy had dropped into the chair by Chambrun's desk:
"Your name is William Chard?"

"Billy. Billy is my name, not William."

"Your address?"

"I don't have a permanent address. I—I've been on
tour with Hilda forever."

"How long is forever?"

"Five, five and a half years," Billy said. "Most of
my personal belongings are in storage. I don't have an
address."

"Where does the government send you your tax
bills?" Hardy asked.

"Do I have to spell it out for you?" Billy almost snarled. "I'm gay, Lieutenant. I wasn't 'in love' with Hilda, but I loved her." He glared at me. "I knew this crazy cocksman would get her into some kind of trouble before we left his gilded whorehouse!"

"What kind of trouble?"

"Hilda was a sexaholic," Billy said. "She forgot about everything that mattered, her career, her health, when she got tangled up with some jerk like Haskell here. When she got through with her act each night she couldn't wait to take off her clothes for some creep. Any creep that was available!"

"She hadn't taken off her clothes tonight when someone strangled her," Hardy said.

"Oh God! What does *he* say?" Billy pointed a shaking finger at me.

"He's pretty well covered, Mr. Chard," Hardy said.

"He would be!"

"He wouldn't be sitting here if he wasn't," Hardy said. "Who else beside Haskell is currently in the lady's life?"

"Whoever groped at her in an elevator," Chard said. His bitterness was painful. "I've told her over and over—someday—some psycho—"

"She told Haskell she was afraid of the man she identified for the police yesterday afternoon. Was he someone she'd—picked up somewhere?"

"No way," Chard said. "She talked about him to me during our show breaks tonight. She was really afraid that character was off his rocker, might come back for some kind of revenge." His eyes widened. "Could it be that way?"

"I can't write it off because I don't have any solid evidence yet," Hardy said. "Was there anyone else staying here in the hotel, or coming to her shows at night, who'd been close to her?"

Chard blotted at his mouth with that handkerchief. It was as if he wanted to wipe away a smile that threatened to appear. "She always talked about her exes—her ex-lovers. She'd come backstage after doing her thing and have a big smile on her face. 'I have three exes out there tonight, Billy,' she'd say."

"She name them?" Hardy asked.

"No. In all the time I've known her she never mentioned a name. She had contempt for those old movie stars who write books about whom they slept with. 'The kiss-and-tell girls,' she called them. But she wasn't very careful either. Anyone working close to her, the way I did, didn't have to guess who the current guy was." He gave me an angry look. "Everyone in this hotel knows it's been Haskell for the last couple of weeks."

"Did she mention there were any other 'exes' in her audience tonight?" Hardy asked.

Chard gave me an odd look, like a scientist who sees something he doesn't understand on his microscope slide. "Haskell had something for her," he said. "One guy for a solid two weeks! That's not like our last stop, which was Washington. We went there for a two-week gig Blue Haven, a jazz spot. Engagement stretched into two months. They really loved Hilda down in our nation's capitol." He let go with his smile at last. "Flying up here, we circled over Washington when we took off—give the sightseers a last look at the sights, I guess. Hilda looked down and gave me a kind of comic grin. 'I sure took that city by storm,' she said. 'Supreme Court, the State Department, the Senate, the House of Representatives, the FBI. About the only place I didn't score, Billy,' she said to me, 'was the White House.' We laughed and I told her, 'If at first you don't succeed . . .'" His smile faded. "We never dreamed she'd never see Washington again."

Jerry Dodd interrupted. "You say she never named names, but can you name some? Washington boy-friends?"

I knew what was on Jerry's mind; Larry Welch's untold story, a fake Martin Stearns who had gotten a message from Welch in Washington. A tie-in could be there.

"I'm not much on names," Chard said. "Those senators and congressmen all look like they came out of the same mold. Me, I have to stop to think what the president's name is. Politics are not my thing."

"She ever mentioned being scared of anyone before? Before this guy she identified for us?" Hardy asked.

"She played by a set of rules," Chard said. "Ask Haskell. She didn't ask for secrets. She didn't get them and she didn't give them. A guy involved with Hilda didn't have to worry about being held up by her. Fun—and variety was all she cared about."

Hardy looked at me. "You buy that, Mark?"

"Fortunately or unfortunately, I don't have any secrets anyone can use against me," I said. "The lady never asked me anything about myself. She enjoyed what we had, and so did I. There wasn't any more to it than that. Fun and games."

"Never any talk about anyone who might have objected to being thrown away like a used candy wrapper?" Hardy asked.

"Never any talk about anyone," I said.

"Never any talk about anyone to me either," Chard said, "and I've been with her for part of every day for the last five and a half years."

"Jealous women? Angry wives?"

"No one, until tonight and that guy she saw messing around on the tenth floor with that elevator operator, and he sure as hell wasn't one of her exes."

So much for the gaudy, reckless, and—some people might think—the tawdry life of Hilda Harding.

"Somebody must know if she has a family somewhere," Hardy said.

"If anybody does, it would be Max," Chard said.

"Max?"

"Max Rosen, her agent."

"I thought he was your agent."

"He was Hilda's agent first. He launched her, made a star of her. He only took me on when I started to work with her. Whatever there is private about Hilda, Max will know it."

"His address and phone number, please," Hardy said.

IT ISN'T EXACTLY flattering to know that you've been just one of a string of scalps hanging in some squaw's war tent. And yet she had been alive and electric and wonderful fun while it lasted. But now she was a police case. Her death, I convinced myself, had nothing to do with what we'd had together. My concerns and my responsibilities had to be for the living. I had to play my part in the game that might save Betsy Ruysdale from something like what had happened to poor Hilda.

Hardy didn't need me. There were acres of ground for him to cover before he could move positively in some hopeful direction—fingerprints, some so-far-overlooked clue, someone who had seen someone moving around the second floor and thought nothing of it at the time, a determination as to whether the lock on my apartment door had been picked by an expert. If the lock had been picked, Hardy had to look for someone with special skills, special hotel habits. If it hadn't been picked, then Hilda must have taken her

killer into my apartment with her, or let him in after
she'd arrived there alone.

I keep saying "he" and "him" because Hardy had
told us that the medical examiner's man reported
Hilda must have been strangled by very large, very
powerful hands—fingers that reached almost around
her neck from front to back.

At five o'clock in the morning, more than twenty
hours since I'd had any sleep, I couldn't go back to my
apartment for rest, or a change of clothes. Police
technicians continued swarming over the place. Still
wearing my dinner jacket, my nighttime uniform on
my job, I got Lucky Lewis to take me up to the top in
the roof car. I could at least bring Chambrun up to
date.

Dim lights showed at the living room windows of
Penthouse 1. Off to the east the first faint signs of
daylight were beginning to show. I have a key to Penthouse 1, a sign that Chambrun trusted me not to use
it if there was any chance of my interrupting something private. I walked through the vestibule and into
Chambrun's living room. For just an instant I felt
something like shock. He was stretched out on the
couch, his head turned to one side, so that, for a moment, I couldn't see his face. The phone, which had an
extra-long cord, had been taken off his desk and put
down on the floor right beside the couch. I moved
quickly around the end of the couch so that I could get

a look at him head-on. He was asleep. God knows he needed it, as did most of us.

I undid my black tie and opened my dress shirt at the collar. I wandered over to the armchair by the French windows and sat down. I thought I'd let Chambrun go a little longer. I could imagine his state of mind, unable to do anything in a world that he normally controlled for fear of endangering Ruysdale, waiting for a phone call that didn't come, which would give him some kind of instructions, make some new demands.

My own eyelids were heavy. The sky in the east was a dark red. "Red in the morning, sailor take warning." We didn't need warnings around here, they were everywhere.

I guess I must have gone off as if I'd been shot between the eyes. Someone was shaking me by the shoulder.

"You haven't got anything better to do than sleep?" Chambrun asked. Then, as I started to stammer some reply, he gave me a weary little smile. "I must have been at it myself when you came in, Mark. When did you come up?"

"Around five." I glanced at my watch. It was just past seven-thirty. I'd picked up a little rest to go on.

"Jerry just called—woke me—to say you could get back into your apartment. The cops are through there."

"Right now I think of it as a chamber of horrors," I said. "If you had seen her—"

"I know," he said. "Jerry has brought me up to date."

"Which is where?" I asked him.

"Nowhere—so far. Dozens of prints to match up, nothing in that department so far. No casuals went up to the second floor, according to Mike Maggio. He was being a little more watchful than usual. The people who have Ruysdale didn't say anything about not watching the second floor. The hotel was full of curious peepers, so Mike was extra careful. The girl went up a little after two. You went up a little after three."

"Has to be someone who came down from up above," I said. "Someone who used the fire stairs. Elevator wouldn't stop at two for them."

Chambrun nodded. "No reason to keep a guard on that floor. Nothing but offices and your apartment, everything locked up. Cleaning people don't hit the offices on two till around four in the morning." He moved away from me. "I put some water through the coffee machine before I woke you. Care for some?"

"I'll get it," I said.

"I'll get it. Don't try moving fast, Mark. You may find it's hell."

He went into his kitchen. I tried stretching and found he was right. Every bone in my body ached. He came back with two mugs of coffee and we sat looking at each other, not talking for a moment or two. The coffee was nectar.

"I don't quite know how to face this day, Mark," Chambrun said. His face had that hard, graven look to it. He brought his fist down on the arm of his chair. "I've fought all kinds of people in my time, from Nazis to street terrorists and psychos roaming around this place of mine—this hotel. I've dealt with punks, and pimps, and drug peddlers, and call girls. I've always faced them head-on, given them no quarter. Now I have to sit still, do nothing, or Ruysdale will have had it. And if I don't sit still, I may be helping someone do in Welch! How do you decide, with any decency or morality, to place one life above another?"

"Welch got into whatever danger he's in knowingly," I said. "He asked you for help through your friend Claude Perrault, but he knew there was danger. He ran his own risks. He knows the situation you're in and he's ready to play ball. Ruysdale is a total victim, boss. She didn't get into anyone's way, she didn't knowingly run any risks. She's being used to bring pressure on you. You have to choose to do what you can for her and wish Larry Welch good luck. You've got Jericho looking out for anything that might explode up here on the roof. What more can you do for him?"

"So I just sit here and let these bastards have their way with Welch? How do I know they'll let Ruysdale go after that? Will it be safe for them to let her go?

Has she seen anyone she can identify for the police? Can she tell us who owns that slightly foreign-sounding voice on the phone? She was right there with him when I taped that call. What do I do, just sit here, go to early mass and pray?"

"It's tough," I said.

"I just don't know how to do nothing!" Chambrun almost shouted.

"But do you know what to *do*, boss?"

He made an almost hysterical gesture toward the roof. "Ten million people out there in that city and not a lead to anyone!"

"Larry Welch," I said.

"Come again?"

"He's got to tell you what it is he's into," I said.

"And if he won't, and I tell him to get out of my hotel, what then?"

"You and Jericho and I should be able to bring a little pressure on him," I said.

Chambrun was on his feet. "You're right, Mark. It's our one chance."

TWO

A FIRST-TIME VISIT to Victoria Haven's penthouse is nothing less than an experience. At first glance you would think it was a hideout for the famous Collier brothers: stacks of yellowing newspapers, books overflowing the bookcases, total disorder, a place snowed under by litter. But a closer examination would show you that there isn't a speck of dust, the place spotlessly clean. And I guess there was a kind of order to the disorder.

"It is," Chambrun once said to me, "a filing cabinet for all the memorable things in a long life. There is everything from a first doll, to love letters, to history as it appeared in the daily press. Ask her for an editorial from the *New York Times* on the day following the end of World War One and she has it. She not only has it, she knows exactly where it is. That place is like a computer, Mark, filled with all the facts about one person's life and everything that even touched the fringes of it."

When Chambrun and I walked out onto his terrace we saw John Jericho sitting on the rim of the little fence that surrounded Victoria Haven's garden. Down below him, at ground level, staring up at him, was Toto.

Jericho waved as we approached. "He thinks he's got me up a tree," he said. "I've been trying to tell him that other people have made the same mistake." He glanced at me. "I see you're dressing for breakfast." He was referring to my rumpled dinner Jacket.

"I can't get into my apartment to change," I said. "Cops."

Jericho slid down off the wall. "Scram, ham!" he said to the dog, and Toto, looking offended, shuffled away. "I don't know what to say to you, Mark. It must have been ghastly for you. Cops getting anywhere?"

"Not so far. They're assuming the man Hilda identified on the tenth floor, the man from the Trapeze, came back to make sure she couldn't pick him out of a lineup if they caught him."

"Nice, easy assumption, isn't it?" Jericho said. "They only have to look for one man for two murders. It could have been two different men, you know. It could have been someone else who did for your girl, Mark, who had nothing whatever to do with the Ballard murder."

"You're the man who doesn't believe in coincidences, John," Chambrun said.

"You're right, I don't," Jericho said. "I've also learned that what appears to be obvious is rarely the answer I'm looking for."

"I've just been telling Mark I can't go through this day just sitting and waiting," Chambrun said. "Welch has to help us. There has to be some kind of lead in the story he's sitting on."

"And we'd better have it before somebody slits his throat," Jericho said.

"Something like that," Chambrun said. "You see, John, I can do exactly what the kidnappers have ordered me to do: I can leave Welch to defend himself, put nothing in the way of their getting to him. But then what? Ruysdale has been gone for more than twenty-four hours. Has she never seen anyone, talked to anyone? We know she was with their spokesman when he put her on the phone with me. Can they ever let her go?"

"I haven't wanted to suggest that to you," Jericho said. "Betsy almost said that on the phone to you, didn't she? Don't worry about her, do what you have to do."

"You gentlemen have such wonderfully resonant voices," Victoria Haven said from the rear door of her penthouse. She stood there, straight and tall, a full-length apron hiding whatever she was wearing under it. She had a pot holder in one hand and a spatula in the other. "If you want to discuss secrets, just know that you can be heard a block away. I was about to put in eggs to go with the bacon. There's enough for all of you. If you're going to throw Betsy Ruysdale to the wolves, you'd better do it on full stomachs."

"It's not a question of abandoning Ruysdale, Victoria," Chambrun said. "It would seem she has no chance, no matter what we do. The only thing we can do is catch up with them and—and—"

"Slit their throats?" the old woman asked. "Your phrase, Jericho."

"Something like that," Jericho said.

"So good-bye, Miss Betsy Ruysdale! It's the way the world is, my dear. Revenge is sweeter than victory." Old Mrs. Haven was pretty damned resonant herself.

Chambrun's eyes were dark and glittering in their deep pouches. "You know of some plan for victory, my dear?"

"It seems to me you have to try, don't you? Pierre?"

"How?"

"We live in a world of plea bargaining," Mrs. Haven said. "So much for so much. Even a monster will make a trade for his own life."

"What do we offer to trade?"

Mrs. Haven looked steadily at the Man. "A life for a life. Or are you too tenderhearted for that, Pierre?"

Jericho leaned forward. "Look, luv, just say what you have on your mind."

"Your instructions are to let people come and go to Penthouse Three without hindrance if you want to see Ruysdale alive again," Mrs. Haven said. "So you do just that! Sooner or later the man will come to force Welch to part with his material, perhaps kill him. With Welch's cooperation you should be able to spot that man. Let him come up to the roof. Between the elevator and Penthouse Three Johnny boy here intercepts him.

"So, I've got him," Jericho said. He was smiling at Mrs. Haven almost patronizingly.

"If he's important enough, you have something to trade," the old lady said.

"And if he doesn't want to be traded?"

Mrs. Haven gave Jericho an impatient look. "If you and Pierre can't persuade him you mean business, you're not the actors I think you are."

"And if he still won't cooperate?" Chambrun asked.

"If it doesn't work, I know what I'd do if someone I cared about was going to be killed, one way or the other," the old lady said. She wasn't kidding, I thought.

"What would you do, Victoria?" Chambrun asked.

Her wide, generous mouth narrowed to a tight slit. "I'd kill him," she said. "What is it, Pierre? Has your blood thinned out? There was once so much talk about the Nazis you killed in the back alleys of Paris."

"And go to jail for the rest of our lives for a lost cause?" Jericho asked.

"You two ought to be smarter than that," Mrs. Haven said. "All kinds of accidents can happen from high places. But if you two are as good as I think you are, it won't come to that. I've always said, Pierre, that you could sell ice to the Eskimos. I think you can persuade this man, if you get him, to make some kind of a trade. Trying would be better than doing nothing, wouldn't it?"

Chambrun and Jericho glanced at each other, and then Chambrun walked over to the old lady and took her hand. He bent down in a courtly gesture and kissed it. "I love you, Victoria," he said.

She gave him a wistful smile. "I'm afraid it's too damned late for that, Pierre," she said.

MUCH LATER I found myself thinking how extraordinary it was for that elegant old lady to have suggested a violence of such proportions. Equally extraordinary—I thought much later—that two sophisticated and cultivated men of the world like Chambrun and Jericho would have even considered it. But pressure of some kind on the enemy, in time, might give Betsy Ruysdale a chance.

Chambrun and Jericho and I walked across to Penthouse 3 after Mrs. Haven had fed us all bacon, eggs, coffee, and hot rolls. We talked of ways and means over that breakfast: how to persuade Larry Welch to come clean, how to cajole him into helping us.

Mrs. Haven, still in that remarkably tough state of mind, had an opinion on that.

"You have a young man whose whole career has been pointed toward a big story that will make him famous forever. He thinks he has it. He's prepared to run any kind of personal risks to pull it off. But..."

"But what, Victoria?" Chambrun asked.

The old lady leaned back in her chair and smiled. "He has a conscience, a commodity most of us don't have," she said. "He won't reveal what he's got without approval from high places. He won't put his country in danger, he won't risk thousands of lives, unless he is reassured that the revelation is vital. I think that conscience will carry over to your Miss Ruysdale, Pierre. I'm not usually wrong about people. Welch is a decent man."

Maybe I've become a cynic, but decent men are hard to come by in the world I know; they don't pass in droves through the Beaumont's lobby. It's a world of rich men, and men who want to become rich men. They are mortal enemies, because you can't add to the number of rich men without making someone a little poorer. The same thing goes for power. There are those in power, and those who plot to overthrow them by violence. You can start out honest and wind up doing anything at all, no matter how underhanded, to get what you want. I remember an old Walt Disney cartoon where the evil fox is looking across the room at the beautiful Miss Millionbucks. There is a close-up of the pupils of his eyes, which have turned into two hearts, pierced by Cupid's arrows. Then the fox takes another look at the beautiful rich girl, smiles a greedy smile, and the bleeding hearts in his eyes turn into dollar signs.

How right was Victoria Haven? How decent would Larry Welch turn out to be?

Larry, in spite of the early hour and a long night, was up and about when Chambrun rang his doorbell. I could hear the TV set going in his living room when he opened the door for us.

"I've just been hearing," he said, nodding toward the living room. "I seem to be responsible for turning all hell loose in your hotel, Mr. Chambrun."

"Maybe you can help us get things back into control," Chambrun said.

"Come in," Larry said. He went to the TV set and turned it off.

In his fancy modern living room Chambrun went directly to the telephone and asked to speak to Ora Veach, the chief operator. "Chambrun here, Miss Veach," he said. "If there is a call for me, I'm in Penthouse Three. Ring once, disconnect, and ring again. If there is a call for Mr. Welch, ring in the normal fashion. Yes. Yours not to reason why, Miss Veach. Thank you." He put down the phone. "If there should be a call from Ruysdale's abductor, I don't want someone else to answer the phone, so he'll know I'm not alone." He took his silver case from his pocket and extracted one of his flat Egyptian cigarettes. He tapped it on the back of his hand. "I have to ask you for your help, Mr. Welch," he said. "Perhaps I should say I have to demand that you help me."

Larry nodded. "I guessed, when I heard the news about Hilda Harding, that you'd be coming. You're going to tell me that I have to give you more information than I have so far."

"You obviously know why, then," Chambrun said.

"Your problems are more important to you than my problems," Larry said. He walked a step or two away from us and then turned back. "You have a murderer or murderers strolling the corridors of your hotel. Your trusted secretary and friend may lose her life whatever you do. You can't stand just sitting back and waiting while some monsters call the turn."

"A perfect analysis," Chambrun said.

"You want names, places."

"And quickly," Chambrun said.

"I don't have names and places that will help you," Larry said. "Please, let me explain."

"I don't want any explanations, I want facts!" Chambrun said.

"Facts that will help you," Larry said. "Let me see what I can do." He drew a deep breath. "A little more than a year ago a man whose name might be 'Smith,' was arrested in the Middle East for selling highly sophisticated radar and weapons technology to leftist terrorists in the Middle East. This Smith was a former employee of the manufacturer of these technologies, had access to secrets that were vital to the nation's defense posture. What he sold to the enemy could set back our chances of staying level with Russia for a whole decade. This is no secret, Mr. Chambrun. After Smith was convicted he was actually interviewed on television by Mike Wallace for CBS's 'Sixty Minutes.' Everybody knew about it—after it was too late. Why did he do it? Why did he jeopardize his country? For money. He wanted to buy a condominium in California and live in comfort.''

"A history lesson isn't going to help me," Chambrun said.

"So you'll understand," Larry said. "Or do you understand already, Mr. Chambrun, that in this day and age patriotism is apt to run a poor second to wealth?"

"Perhaps not for everyone," Chambrun said.

"Perhaps not for you, or Jericho, or Mark—or me," Larry said. "Let me go on. After the 'Smith' case was over and done, your friend and mine, Claude Perrault, working for the French Sûreté, learned that highly important French technology was leaking into the hands of a Middle Eastern terrorist whose name is Rhamadir. Rhamadir is armed by the Russians, supported by the Russians, and paid for that support with technological information he was buying from French traitors, along with even more important information he was buying from American traitors. Perrault put me on the track of it, a few leads to the American end of the treachery. I've spent almost a year working at it. I've come up with enough evidence against a man working in the Middle East to hang him."

"His name," Chambrun said.

"I'm going to tell you his name," Larry said, "and pray that you'll keep it off the record for now. If we close in on him too soon, others will escape. What I needed from Martin Stearns—and the two men who are coming here today—is a judgment on timing."

"His name!" Chambrun almost shouted.

"His name is Alex Johnson," Larry said, quietly. "He is a government agent working under cover, we thought, but actually dealing with the enemy. What is called a double agent. He is being supplied with what he sells by American, French, and West German traitors. Those suppliers are the men we still haven't enough on to act. Close in on Alex Johnson before we're ready, and the others can slip through our net. What I have in that briefcase is the evidence against Johnson, dug out by Claude Perrault and me, plus leads to his suppliers—but not quite enough yet. Problem—do we shut down on Johnson now, leaving the rest of his network intact, or do we let him go on selling more and more secrets to the enemy, weakening our position vis-à-vis Russia, so that we can crack the whole machine? That's a judgment I can't make. That's why Stearns and these other men are coming here to see me, to help make that decision."

"Are you trying to tell us that this Alex Johnson is responsible for Betsy Ruysdale's kidnapping?" Jericho asked.

"Johnson probably never heard of your Miss Ruysdale," Larry said. "But he's heard of me, and he's heard of Claude Perrault. I wish to God we could reach Claude, Chambrun. He may be in bigger trouble than I am. France is crawling with terrorists, Arab leftists, anti-Israeli people."

"We're apparently crawling with something of the same kind here," Jericho said. "So what are the names of the traitors you have here?"

"In New York, nobody," Larry said, "except that they may be back and forth. United Nations here, the heart of the financial world here. Washington is a key place. Defense factories all over the country are key places."

"Names!" Chambrun said.

"That's the dynamite I talked about once," Larry said. "I give you any of those names, and you move against any one of them, and the whole ball game is lost. The rest of them will take cover. Alex Johnson will take cover, and it will take months and months to get back on the trail of treachery."

"There is Ruysdale!" Chambrun said.

"I've thought about her, and thought," Larry said. "Will they let her go, no matter what you do? The people whose names I might give you are not holding her, Chambrun. One of them may have given the orders, but the people who are holding her are just plain gunmen, paid terrorists. X, Y, and Z—they just carry out orders, and those orders are that if there is a ripple on the surface of the water, here in the Beaumont, Miss Ruysdale has seen her last sunrise. The men holding her kill for money, not for a cause."

"Name us a name of someone who might give orders, we put the heat on him, and those orders might be changed," Jericho said.

"Put the heat on one of them, and that heat will be felt from here to Teheran, to Alex Johnson, to Rhamadir in the time it takes to make an overseas phone call," Larry said. "Not only will Ruysdale get what they plan for her, but the whole network will slip through our fingers." He looked at Chambrun. "I'd like it if you could understand, Mr. Chambrun, that I'm not holding out to make some sort of headlines for myself. If I thought that naming someone would save your Miss Ruysdale, I'd do it. But it's not a story that's at stake, it's the future safety of our country." He looked steadily at Chambrun. "You still want me to name some names that may or may not be useful?"

Chambrun had a kind of frozen look to him. "You have no idea who the man is who's been drinking in the Trapeze the last few days, Ballard's probable murderer?" he asked.

"I've never seen him, only the police artist's drawing," Larry said. "From that I have to say no."

We had come here so ready to "go," but Larry Welch seemed to have persuaded us that to go was too dangerous for all concerned.

"I've got one more for you, Welch," Jericho said. "Neither Chambrun nor I believe in coincidence. Hilda Harding identified the man we think may be Bob Ballard's killer. The present wild-eyed theory is that this man came back here to kill Miss Harding so she couldn't identify him all over again if he was caught. Does that sound like a kill for-a-buck man?"

"Just some kind of a psycho," Welch said.

"Are you suggesting that Ballard's murder didn't have anything to do with you?" Jericho asked.

"I didn't see a connection at first," Larry said. "But after Prescott found out the man who visited me *wasn't* Martin Stearns..."

"Of course," Jericho said. "You call down and tell Ballard on the elevator he's to come up and take down Martin Stearns. Ballard, a piece of bad luck for your fake visitor, has worked in the office building where the real Stearns is located in Washington. He comes up, opens the car door, expecting to see a familiar face. Instead he sees a stranger, says, 'You're not Martin Stearns,' and finds himself facing a gun. He's ordered to stop at the tenth floor, is forced off the car and shoved into the service area, where he's killed."

"Where does the man from the Trapeze come in if my fake Stearns was the killer?" Larry asked.

"A riddle," Jericho said with a grim smile.

"Planted on the tenth floor, just in case?" Larry suggested. "He's there to take Ballard off the car when it stops. Miss Harding sees him, goes back into her room. The fake Stearns gets off the car and walks away unnoticed?"

"Meanwhile the dark man, Mr. X, shoots Ballard, stuffs him in a trash can, and goes down to the Trapeze to buy himself a vodka and tonic, knowing he's been seen?" Chambrun's laugh was mirthless. "You have a fiction writer's talent, Mr. Welch."

"So what did happen?" Larry asked.

"A riddle," Jericho said.

"I am going to insist on some names, Mr. Welch," Chambrun said. "You have told us two men were coming here today to advise you. Who are they?"

"I—I can't tell you that," Larry said.

"If you don't tell me," Chambrun said, "they're not going to get up here to see you. Understand, if I give the orders, no one is going to get up here, and no one can get down from here—and that means you—unless I say so. This is one place I can control."

"Why would you want to keep them from coming?" Larry asked.

"I will not let people walk into a trap set up by the people who have Ruysdale. I have let two people be killed by playing their games—thinking it might save Ruysdale. No more. Tell me who they are. Phone them in my presence and warn them what they may be facing. If they want to run the risk, that will be their decision."

"Both men are traveling to get here," Larry said. "I have no way to reach them on the way."

"You know them both?"

"One of them I know well. The other I know all about, but I've never seen or met him."

"Names, please. Because no one is going to get up here until I'm satisfied they are who they are supposed to be. You may be a very clever man, Mr. Welch, but you've been faked out once and it's cost two lives. Not again."

Larry hesitated a moment. He had to know that Chambrun could no longer be counted on to sit back and do nothing. "The man I know is Armand Beaujon, a friend of Claude Perrault's. He works for French security. The man I don't know is Michael O'Brien, an Irishman working for British security."

"Why are these men important to you?"

"I've told you."

"You've hinted. Tell me." This was the hanging judge.

Larry seemed to make a decision. "There are three key people working for Alex Johnson and Rhamadir in the Middle East," he said. "One of them is a discredited CIA man from this country; one is a Frenchman, a former Foreign Legion officer; and the third is an Irishman, an IRA man driven into exile by the British. How dangerous would it be to reveal their names? Claude Perrault and I felt we must have advice because to name them could mean their source of information, their suppliers of technological secrets, could slip out of the net. How ready are the governments of the United States, France, and Britain to pounce? Martin Stearns was supposed to supply me with an answer for America. Armand Beaujon will advise us about France. Michael O'Brien knows the Irish terrorists inside out, and can advise about Britain's position."

"The man you thought was Martin Stearns advised you to do nothing, to ditch your story," Jericho said.

"Naturally. He was a fake," Chambrun said. "So you will pay no attention to that. You say you know this Beaujon and trust him."

"A lot of the material I have came from him in the first place," Larry said. "It's a matter of when it's safe to break the story."

"O'Brien?"

"An Irishman working for the British?" Jericho sounded unconvinced.

"My dear fellow, all over the world Frenchmen and Americans and Germans and British and, for God's sake, even Chinese are working for the Russians. In turn, Russians are working for all of us. It isn't where a man is born that matters. It's what he believes, or, more likely, how much money he can make working for the other side."

"To paraphrase the late Sam Goldwyn," Jericho said, "George Washington would turn over in his grave if he was alive! Patriotism would seem to be up the creek!"

"And out of sight in most places," Larry said.

"So let's look at it carefully," Chambrun said. "The man you thought was Martin Stearns advised you to forget what you have. Now that you know he was a fake you'll still wait for the real Martin Stearns's opinion?"

Larry nodded.

"You will accept what this Beaujon has to tell you. You know him, know him by sight."

"Yes."

"But O'Brien. How will you make sure of him? He can have passport and driver's license, with his pictures. They can be as phony as the Stearns fakes were."

Larry frowned. "Beaujon would know him."

"Can you keep Beaujon here till O'Brien arrives?"

"I don't know."

"I can keep him here whether he likes it or not," Chambrun said. "All you have to do is tell Beaujon what's happened and what could be going to happen, and if he's so damned concerned with his country and its secrets, he'll stay."

"Probably."

"He'll stay!" Chambrun said. "Your way or mine. Here's how we're going to play it, Mr. Welch. Jericho will be painting Mrs. Haven out in her garden. When Beaujon arrives not only will you be notified by the car operator, but I will be notified and so will Jericho. You will come out in the open, onto the roof, to greet Beaujon. If he is certainly the man you know, you will signal Jericho. Understood?''

"Yes."

"You will explain to Beaujon what the situation is and ask him to stay till O'Brien, whom he knows, arrives. If he insists on leaving, you will walk out onto the roof with him and signal to Jericho again. He won't leave, because no car will come up for him, and Jericho will handle him if he makes trouble."

"In spades and with pleasure," Jericho said.

"So when O'Brien comes, we'll check him out as best we can in the lobby level. If he seems for real, the operator will bring him up if you give the word. You and Beaujon will come out on the roof to greet him. If Beaujon says he's legitimate, you'll signal to Jericho again."

"And if he isn't—and if he's armed?" Larry asked.

Jericho patted a bulge I hadn't noticed on the left side of his jacket. "I've won prizes at target shooting with a handgun," he said.

THREE

CHAMBRUN AND JERICHO, with Larry Welch's help, were prepared for action that might be coming up on the roof. But the world was turning in other directions. So often I've heard Chambrun excuse himself with "I've got a hotel to run." Today he wouldn't free himself for ordinary routines. There might be some word from the kidnappers, although they had said they would not call again. Ruysdale, who could have handled the daily functioning of the Beaumont with the same Swiss-watch efficiency as the Man, was missing. My normal morning involved checking the list of guests who'd registered since yesterday, always with Chambrun and Ruysdale after the Man's breakfast. Not today. The purpose of checking that list was to determine who needed special attention. There could be a film star who wanted to stay anonymous, there could be another film star or a foreign dignitary who wanted the reverse treatment: red carpet out, drum and bugle corps. It was my job to hide or exploit. But that was not for today either.

When I got down to the second floor and my apartment to change out of the dinner clothes I'd been wearing for nearly twelve hours, I found a uniformed cop standing guard out in the hall.

"We're through in there, Mr. Haskell," he told me. "Bit of a mess until whoever cleans for you can get to it. I've been waiting here to tell you the lieutenant wants you up in the victim's room on the tenth floor as soon as you can make it."

"As soon as I get out of my ball gown," I said. I thought that was funny, but I'm not sure the cop did.

Believe it or not, I'd never been in the room Hilda had occupied on ten. It was like a hundred other single rooms in the hotel. My place had been more comfortable for our purposes. Hardy was in 1006 with Officer Moncrief, the stenotype operator, and a slim, dark, ferret-faced man who turned out to be Max Rosen, Hilda and Billy Chard's agent.

"I guess none of us had had a day like this before," Rosen said to me when he was introduced. He looked pretty well shaken up.

"Mr. Rosen has been telling me some things about Hilda Harding," the lieutenant said. "You say you never talked about anything but making love, Mark, but surely there must have been some chitchat about other things."

"So help me," I said, "the weather—maybe something about the news we heard on the radio when I was getting up in the morning."

"She ever talk to you about her brother?"

"I didn't know she had a brother," I said. "No, she never mentioned him."

"Stanislaus Wolenski," Rosen said. "Big wheel in Poland when the Solidarity people there were riding high. When the military took over, Stan disappeared, like a lot of other Solidarity leaders. Hilda's been trying for two years to find some trace of him."

"But no luck?"

Rosen shook his head. "It had an effect on her career," he said. "She insisted I get her bookings in foreign capitals in Europe, later in Washington." His narrow little mouth moved in a bitter downtwist. "She thought she had a way to charm people in high places to tell her something that would help her find her brother."

"In other words, she went to bed with the right people," Hardy said. He sounded as if he'd tasted something he didn't like.

"That's how it was, I think," Rosen said.

Hardy looked at me. "I don't imagine you have any pull with the Polish authorities, do you, Mark? Mr. Rosen wondered."

"I only know one or two Polish jokes," I said.

"But there are people in this hotel, people at the United Nations, people from Washington. She ever ask you about any of them, try to get you to introduce her to any of them?"

"No. I guess I flattered myself into thinking she was just interested in me as a man."

Hardy gave me a faint smile. "It could be, I suppose. A man who could send flowers like that! Must have cost you a week's wages.'' He motioned toward the dressing table at the far end of the room. For the first time I noticed a tall vase of beautiful long-stemmed American-beauty roses.

''What makes you think I sent her those flowers,'' I said. ''I didn't, as a matter of fact.''

Hardy frowned. ''Says so on the card,'' he said. He crossed over and picked up a card that was propped against the vase. He handed it to me.

The card was from the Beaumont florists, located in the lobby. The message was typed on it, indicating that the order had come over the phone, someone in the shop typing on the words someone had given them. ''A token of my eternal gratitude, M.''

''I knew you'd stood her up for lunch. I thought you'd decided to buy forgiveness. M for Mark.''

''Not me,'' I said. I glanced at Rosen. ''M for Max,'' I suggested.

''Is the florist open now, ten after nine?'' Hardy asked.

''Should be.''

''Get them on the phone and ask them who ordered the flowers,'' he said.

I know the people in the florist shop. I buy flowers there from time to time, order them for other guests of the hotel. The clerk who answered the phone is one Jean Potts, a not unattractive girl.

"It's Mark Haskell, Jean," I said. "I want to inquire about some flowers that were sent to Hilda Harding in 1006, sometime yesterday."

"Oh, my, Mark, we've just been hearing. How awful."

"The message with the flowers was typed, which means the order was phoned in, doesn't it?"

"Yes, I don't remember the order. It must have come late in the day. I'm off at five o'clock. Let me check the records." She was gone for a minute or two and when she came back she sounded strange. "The flowers were ordered about eight in the evening, Mark. The message was 'A token of my eternal gratitude. M.'"

"Who ordered them?"

"Why—why you did, Mark. They've been charged to your account."

"Now wait a minute—who took the order?"

"Laura Collins—she's relatively new on the night shift."

"How do we reach her?"

"Hold on, there's a home phone for her here." She gave me a number.

A few minutes later I had Laura Collins on the phone. I told her who I was and that I was interested in an order of flowers for Hilda Harding.

"Oh, dear, Mr. Haskell, I hope nothing went wrong with them."

"Oh, they were delivered," I said. "You been listening to your radio?"

"No. I haven't."

"Well, when we get through turn it on. You'll understand then why I'm concerned. I didn't order those flowers, Laura."

"But you called! A dozen American beauties to be delivered to Miss Harding's room, not her dressing room in the Blue Lagoon. You gave me the message to go with them!"

"You're talking to me now, Laura. Did the voice on the phone sound like me?"

"Oh, gee, Mr. Haskell, I—I just took it for granted it was you. You said, 'Put it on my special account.'"

"It wasn't me, luv," I said. "So, turn on your radio and brace yourself."

I reported the conversation to Hardy.

"Can anyone just call in and give a name, no credit card, or anything like that?"

"I can," I said. "I order flowers all the time, for special parties, for guests to whom we want to give a special welcome, for stars appearing in the Blue Lagoon, like Hilda. My special account is for flowers I order for which the hotel will pick up the tab."

"So this 'M' knew how to send some flowers to the lady for free," Hardy said.

"If he said 'special account' to Laura Collins on the phone, she had no reason to doubt it was me," I said. "You could call those 'code words.' I don't remember ever talking to her on the phone. Usually I go into the shop to see what I'm buying. She wouldn't necessarily be sure of my voice. I don't stammer or say 'ain't,' or anything distinctive like that.''

"She must have had another lover in the hotel," Max Rosen said.

"That would have made her schedule pretty damn crowded," I said. I meant it to be funny, but as I said it I felt a little twinge of pain. Whatever Hilda's history might be, as told by Billy Chard and this Rosen character, I knew the time she'd spent with me had been just exactly what it seemed to be. She'd never asked me a question about anyone, never tried to get any kind of special favor from me, never even shown any interest in my background, my family, my schooling, any other women in my past, my yesterdays. That had been one of the special things about her. She was only interested in *now*, in the exact moment she was living; in our case the number of volts of electricity we could generate together. I've got to say the needle on the face of the dial must have quivered when we got going. She had been so spectacular. The anger I'd felt some hours ago when I'd first seen Hilda lying on my bed, her lovely face turned into a grotesque mask, began cooking again. If I could get my hand on the bastard who'd choked her life away, I'd—I'd..."

Hardy was thanking Rosen for coming in, telling him he could go. Rosen was assuming he'd have to make the funeral arrangements when the medical examiner released the body.

"Cremation, of course," Rosen said. "She wouldn't want anyone to see her the way she is now."

The same thought I'd had when I'd covered her face with the towel after I'd found her.

"Memorial service somewhere," Rosen was saying. "God, Madison Square Garden wouldn't hold half the fans who'll want to pay their respects."

I started to leave with Rosen, but Hardy asked me to stay with him. When Rosen had gone he told me what was on his mind.

"The lock on the door to your apartment wasn't picked, Mark," he said. "That limits the possibilities. Either you left it unlocked, she left it unlocked after she got there, or she took someone with her or let someone in after she got there. No one forced their way in."

"I didn't leave it unlocked. To begin with, you don't have to lock it; it has a Yale-type lock that works automatically when you close the door. It's as automatic with me as taking my next breath to close the door when I leave, and then test it to make sure. You ask me if I remember doing it and I have to tell you no, no more than I recall remembering to breathe. But I did it."

"There've been a lot of dames in your life over your years here, Mark. Did any one of them ever take off with a key you'd let them have?"

"No. That I'd remember."

"So the only keys are the one you carry and the one you gave the Harding girl?"

"And one in the key locker in the front office."

"The maid who cleans up for you?"

"Oh, she has a key."

"You see, keys multiply when you begin talking about them," Hardy said.

"No way to get the key from the key locker," I said. "The maid has been here longer than I have, totally trustworthy."

"We'll check out her routines," Hardy said. "Now, once more, who did the Harding girl know who lives in the hotel, or circulates here?"

"No one and everyone," I said. "She is—was—no different from any star performer. Everyone knows who she is, people speak to her, she answers. She had a table reserved in the Blue Lagoon for between-shows. She'd come out and sit—have a white wine on the rocks, maybe—and people would flock around her, for autographs, just for conversation, to be warmed by that marvelous smile of hers."

"No one in particular? No reporters?"

"Hell, yes, there were reporters! But not anyone I thought of as special. I—I thought I was the special person in her life just now."

Hardy, like a bull terrier, wouldn't let go. "Would she be likely to take some guy up to your apartment for fun and games?" he asked.

"I'd say no, never. She had this room, her own room, for something like that," I said, and was certain of it.

"So she took someone to your apartment—or let someone in after she got there—someone she thought had a right to be there. A friend of yours? Your night bell captain, Maggio, knew she was up there—arranged to have the elevator let her out at two. I understand they call him 'the Italian stallion' around the hotel. Could he have been poaching on your territory? He knew he'd have time before you showed up."

"You're dreaming," I said. I felt impatient with him. "Mike is one of the people here I'd trust to the limit. Chambrun feels that way about him, too."

"*M* could stand for 'Mike,'" he said, glancing at the flowers.

"Those roses were ordered at eight o'clock," I said. "Mike didn't know Hilda was going up to my place till around two in the morning."

"Didn't he know that she was going up to your place every night? He goes up to your place, knocks on the door, tells her he has a message from you, and he's in."

"I won't buy that now, Hardy, or ever," I said.

"I'll do some checking," he said.

METHODICAL CHECKING is Hardy's special gift as a detective. He will follow any lead—no matter how farfetched—right to the end of the line until it proves out one way or another. Mike Maggio was in for a very close looking-at, I knew. In the end Hardy would clear him, because I would have bet my life on Mike's integrity. What I couldn't guess just then was that Mike would play a key part in the capture of a killer.

That capture seemed far away to me that morning. I wanted it so badly I could taste it. All the jive I'd heard about Hilda in the last hours didn't make her any less deserving of justice. But the key concern of the moment had to be Ruysdale and the cat-and-mouse games going on up on the Beaumont's roof. If one of the men Larry Welch was expecting today turned out to be a phony, then Chambrun and Jericho could hope they might find themselves in a position to deal.

I couldn't wait to get back up to the roof to see what happened when Welch's first visitor arrived. Down in the lobby I approached the roof car. Dick Berger was at his usual post, looking tight lipped and grim. Overnight his job on the roof car had become a high-risk assignment. Bob Ballard had wound up dead, stuffed into a trash can.

"No callers for the roof so far this morning," he told me. "Comings and goings: Jerry Dodd, you, Mrs. Kniffin—the head housekeeper—a couple of night elevator men from this south bank of cars. Busy but tranquil. I hope it stays that way. Chambrun playing detective, I guess, questioning people."

Dick took me up to the roof. The first thing I saw when I got up there was old Mrs. Haven sitting in her garden, wearing a wide-brimmed straw garden hat. Jericho was nearby, canvas on an easel, apparently beginning his painting.

Chambrun was still in his living room, pacing restlessly. Welch's first visitor, Armand Beaujon, would be coming very soon. I crossed to the French windows to look at the artist at work again.

"Why is she wearing that hat?" I asked. "He can't see her face under that brim."

Chambrun managed a smile. "It's the color of her hair," he said. "There is no such color! Jericho can't reproduce it, so I guess he's suggested the hat."

"It is a hot August morning," I said.

"Have it your way," Chambrun said. He'd lost interest.

"Dick Berger says you've had Mrs. Kniffin and a couple of the night elevator men up here," I said.

"People who might have noticed anyone on the second floor who shouldn't have been there," Chambrun said.

"Anything?"

"This is not a day when anything is ready to go our way," Chambrun said. "Hardy used my office, cops back and forth; Hilda Harding, Prescott, who was using my phone to try to locate the real Martin Stearns, Jerry Dodd. No one clocked anybody, except Mike Maggio, who had times for Hilda and you."

I told him about the flowers that had been charged to my expense account and Hardy's dreams about Mike. He listened, frowning.

"I trust Maggio all the way," he said.

"I told Hardy that."

There were two short rings on the little phone that connected with the roof car. I was nearest it, and reached for it.

"Don't pick it up!" Chambrun said. His eyes were suddenly very bright. "I told Dick Berger to ring me twice when Welch had a visitor. I told him I wouldn't answer. I didn't want the visitor knowing that anyone but Welch had been contacted."

We went out onto the terrace and Chambrun gave Jericho some kind of prearranged signal. The big artist left his easel and went around to the side of Penthouse 2.

Welch came out of Penthouse 3 and stood facing the canopy over the elevator door. This was going to be something or nothing. My heart began to beat a tattoo in my chest.

The elevator door opened and a tall, dark-haired man emerged. He was wearing a dark blue tropical worsted suit and carrying a briefcase. He looked around, spotted Larry Welch, and walked quickly toward him. I could see Welch smiling. He waved at Jericho. This was obviously the real Armand Beaujon.

We watched him go into Penthouse 3 with Larry.

"Do you know," I heard Chambrun say softly, "I almost wish he had been a fake. This means waiting till afternoon for the next one. I don't know if I can take it, Mark. What can they be doing to Ruysdale? Damn them! Damn, damn, damn!"

"We can just hope Beaujon agrees to play ball and wait for O'Brien to come," I said.

"He'll stay here, that I promise you!" Chambrun said.

The roof-car phone was ringing when we got back inside. This time Chambrun answered. Dick Berger was calling to say that Mike Maggio wanted to come up and see the Man. He was given the all-clear.

"He's probably coming to tell me Hardy's off his rocker," Chambrun said. "I don't need to be reassured about Maggio."

Mike was off duty, of course, at ten in the morning, but Jerry Dodd had asked him to stay aboard in case extra help was needed. He could be used as a replacement for Bob Ballard on the roof car, 3:00 to 11:00 P.M.

Mike came off the elevator. He was whistling as he crossed the patio to Chambrun's place. Off duty, he was wearing his own style clothes, a short-sleeved plaid sports shirt, blue jeans, sneakers. He was a muscular, well-built young man who looked as if he'd spent a lot of his free time at the beaches. He was mahogany brown.

As I greeted him at the door of Chambrun's place he grinned at me, holding up his hands, palms out, in a gesture of surrender. "You may search me," he said.

"Search you?"

"For hidden weapons. Have you heard that Mr. C.'s crazy friend downstairs has got me near the top on his list of suspects?"

"Hardy?"

"Or maybe he's picking on me because he doesn't have any suspects, got to make himself look good with his top brass. But I've got an alibi." Mike laughed. "The girl wasn't raped before she was killed. That clears me." He stopped dead in his track and the look on his face was almost comic. "Oh, Jesus, Mark, I'm sorry. How stupid can I be, saying something like that in front of you? I'm a little sore at Hardy, and I guess I was just trying to laugh it off." He stuck his chin out. "Take a whack at it if you want, pal."

"Forget it," I said.

"And don't waste time being 'sore' at Hardy," Chambrun said. He'd come up behind us. "He's good at his job because he doesn't brush off even the most unlikely lead."

"You know how it is, Mr. C. Not me! You, Mark—okay. But not *me!* That's crazy!"

"Come in, Mike," the Man said. "I assume you've been playing detective and want to tell me about it."

"Everybody on the staff is playing detective," Mike said. "Bob Ballard was liked. And Miss Harding, she never gave any of us the 'big-star' treatment. Nice lady." He glanced at me. "Until she came here and Mark took up all her time, she just about played the field from one end to the other. I understand she excused it on the grounds she was looking for a brother who's dead or in Siberia."

"Word seems to get around," Chambrun said.

"She's just come from a couple of months in Washington," Mike said. "Stayed at the Wyndham. Fellow who has my job down there is an old friend. I called him to ask him what the gossip is. I thought maybe somebody she spent time with down there could be hanging around here."

"Interesting thought," Chambrun said.

"The bastard who did her in sure as hell hated her for some reason," Mike said. "I came up with two names, one of which you'll get a laugh on."

"It'll have to be awfully funny for me to start laughing," Chambrun said.

"My friend at the Wyndham says she had half the big shots in Washington on her string—judges, senators, the works. I'm sorry Mark, but that's the story."

"I've heard it before," I said.

"Well, the first name I got is Guy Morton," Mike said. "Covers the United Nations for a Washington newspaper. You know him, boss. He stays here when the U.N. is in session. He's been in the Blue Lagoon damn near every night since the lady's been here, taking in her act, joining her at her table between shows."

"Last night?" Chambrun asked.

"He wasn't in the Lagoon last night," Mike said. "But I saw him come into the lobby a little after midnight and go straight to the elevators. His room is on the twenty-sixth floor."

"He could have come back down to two," I said.

"Anybody *could* have come down to two," Mike said. "Not on the elevators, though. Two was crawling with cops."

"Not till after the lady was killed," Chambrun said.

"Except for a friend of yours who was back and forth, Mr. C. And this is what I said would give you a laugh. One of Hilda's boyfriends in the Wyndham in Washington was Mitchell Prescott."

Chambrun didn't laugh. His forehead was scarred by a deep frown.

Mike laughed as if to try to get the humor going. "Hardy mentioned the flowers someone sent the lady last night—on your account, Mark! I've got him dizzy with that. 'A token of my eternal gratitude. M.' He started playing with *M* is for 'Mark,' and *M* is for 'Mike.' I gave him *M* is for 'Morton,' and *M* is for 'Mitch,' Hardy's like a one-armed juggler, playing with those." That didn't raise a laugh. "I saw Morton take off for the U.N. this morning and there wasn't a sign of blood on his hands!" That didn't get a laugh either.

Instead Chambrun turned to me and told me to ask Jericho and Mrs. Haven to join us.

"You want me to go, boss?" Mike asked.

"Yes, Mike. And thank you for coming up. If Hardy really gets difficult, let me know."

I walked across the roof to Mrs. Haven's garden. "Chambrun wants you two to join him," I said.

"He's heard something?" Jericho asked.

"Who knows what he hears," I said.

"I'll go as far as his terrace," Jericho said. "I don't want to be cut out of sight if Welch doesn't persuade his guest to stay."

We went back to Chambrun's place, under the awning that covers his terrace. I told Chambrun that Jericho didn't want to have Penthouse 3 out of sight.

"Two heads are better than one," Chambrun said. "Let's join him."

Mrs. Haven was sitting in a wicker armchair. She'd taken off her garden hat and was fanning herself with it. Looking at her gaudy red hair, I realized Chambrun was right. There *is* no such color. Jericho stood at the edge of the terrace, looking down across the roof to Penthouse 3.

Chambrun brought them up to date: the reports we'd had on Hilda's life-style from Max Rosen; the flowers that had been ordered by phone, using my name, and sent to Hilda's room; and, finally, Mike's report on what he'd learned from the bell captain at the Wyndham in Washington.

"One thing we have to say for the late Miss Harding," Jericho said, "she bestowed her favors on people who could really help her in her search for her brother if they would. Guy Morton knows everyone worth knowing in the world of international diplomacy—both sides of the fence, friend or enemy. Mitch Prescott has all the resources of the CIA at his disposal."

"And Mark Haskell didn't have anything to offer, and wasn't asked for anything," I heard myself say with a touch of anger. No scheming in my world.

Mrs. Haven gave me a gentle smile, an older person to a kid who was out of line. "You have money in the bank, Mark, you can spend it for necessities, and you can spend it for just sheer pleasure. I'm sure you provided Hilda with something that she cherished." She looked out at the hazy summer sunshine. "There was a time in my life when I used what I had to offer both ways." Then she actually giggled. "But can you imagine Mitch Prescott—in his Brooks Brothers suit, his Dunhill pipe—and that very glamorous young woman!"

"You know him, Victoria?"

"Of course," Mrs. Haven said. "I mean, he lives here when he's in town. Somebody introduced me to him in the Trapeze a few years ago. He often comes over to my table. We chat about what's going on in the world, places where we've both spent time in Europe, particularly the south of France. There's a little pension in Cannes where—"

"Let's touch a few bases," Chambrun interrupted her. "The whole New York City police force is looking for that character who has been drinking one vodka and tonic in the Trapeze for the last few days. Who first called him to our attention? Mitch Prescott, asking Mark about him. Who had him identified for the police as Bob Ballard's killer? Mitch Prescott's former girl friend. Who had access to the second floor, where that girl was killed, could come and go without arousing any suspicion? Mitch Prescott, who was using my office as a base for making phone calls in an effort to locate the real Martin Stearns. And—*M* could stand for 'Mitch.' She did him a favor, for which he was grateful."

"You don't know that," Mrs. Haven said.

"*M* could stand for 'Mitch,'" Jericho said.

"Grateful and then killed her?" Mrs. Haven asked. "Aren't you reaching pretty far, Pierre?"

"A lot of coincidences have a way of adding up," Chambrun said.

"It seems to me you have a simple approach," Mrs. Haven said. "The police have taken fingerprints from all over Mark's apartment. Tell Hardy what you suspect, and he'll take Mitch's prints and match them up. If they match, you've solved the case. If they don't— well, then you start over."

"One of the things that surprises me about you, Victoria," Chambrun said, "is that you often don't think things through to the end of the line."

She smiled at him. "So I'm still in the suburbs. Guide me into town."

"Ruysdale!" Chambrun said. "If Prescott is part of that and we even nod our heads in his direction, Ruysdale will pay for it."

"And you've already said, Pierre, that even if you do nothing, Ruysdale won't be set free," Mrs. Haven said. "Would it help you to be surer about Prescott? Why not ask Larry Welch if Prescott is one of the names he hasn't wanted to mention. How much better located could an American traitor be than in the CIA?"

"I think, my fair lady," Jericho said, "the fact is Pierre doesn't need anything more to convince him about Prescott. The door to Mark's apartment wasn't forced, the lock wasn't picked. Prescott is around the second floor. The girl meets him, invites him in for a conversation. He's grateful for a favor she did him, let us say 'out of bed.' Now she lets him know she wants to be paid for that favor. He can't afford the price and 'Good-night lady!'"

"You and Pierre ought to be writing soap operas," Mrs. Haven said. "You're far more imaginative than their regular people. What about Guy Morton?"

"He's an also-ran," Jericho said. "He couldn't have been wandering around the second floor without being noticed."

"The Harding girl could have taken him up with her."

"But she didn't. Mike Maggio and Company would have noticed."

"So you've convinced me," Victoria Haven said. She gave her straw hat a twirl and put it back on her head. "You've also convinced me you can't do anything about it without endangering Miss Ruysdale. All you can do is wait and watch. So, let's get back to work, Jericho."

Jericho didn't move. "Ruysdale," he said quietly, "one way or the other. She's alive because they may need her to convince Pierre to keep playing ball their way. When they don't need him anymore?..." Jericho shrugged his huge shoulders. "I vote for a collision course." He looked steadily at Chambrun. I had a feeling the plan they'd already discussed in terms of Larry Welch's possible fake guest was being considered by Jericho for Mitchell Prescott.

Mrs. Haven seemed to be in on it, too. "If you're wrong about Prescott, it can't do any harm," she said. "If you're right?..."

"When you have to gamble," Jericho said, "you have to risk losing. But if you're going to lose anyway if you don't gamble, you don't have much of a choice."

Chambrun sat with his hands raised to his mouth, as though that would hide some kind of weakness. He was being torn apart by a decision he had to make. He lowered those hands.

"So be it," he said. He stood up. "Mark, see if you can locate Prescott somewhere in the hotel."

"If he's an honest man, he will have gone to work," Victoria Haven said.

"When you find him, Mark," Chambrun said, ignoring the old woman's comment, "ask him, very politely, if he'd mind coming up here for a few minutes—that I need his help."

Mrs. Haven gave me a sweet smile. "You can't hang a man, Mark, unless he's present for the occasion."

I DON'T quite know now, long afterwards, exactly what I was feeling when I set out to find Mitch Prescott. All the talk had sounded reasonable enough, added up, certainly, to grounds for suspicion, and yet I think I simply couldn't swallow the idea that this man, this citizen, this important citizen, whom I'd known as a guest of the Beaumont for some years, could possibly be a traitor to his country, a kidnapper, and a murderer! Not good old Mitch, with his pleasant smile, his expensive wardrobe, his reassuring pipe. I think I remembered some old advertisement about "You can trust a man who smokes a pipe," Doctor Watson's Cube-Cut Burley. I'd had drinks with him, passed jokes with him, provided him with special little services for a special guest. Not Mitch! I think I may have had some uncomfortable fantasies about good old Mitch enjoying himself in the hay with

Hilda. And then killing her? It just wasn't for real—not just then.

I found him, and instantly thought of Mrs. Haven's remark that if he were an honest man, he'd be at work. He was sitting in the Grill Room, a silver coffeepot and a cup at his elbow, a copy of the *Times* propped up in front of him, his pipe providing a little halo of smoke around his bald head. When I spoke he looked up at me over the top of the half-glasses he wore for reading.

"Mark," he said, "my dear fellow. What a ghastly business for you." He gestured toward the paper. "Join me? I'll order some more coffee."

"I was actually looking for you," I said. "Chambrun wonders if you'd mind coming up to his penthouse. He says he needs your help with something."

"More about Martin Stearns?" he asked.

"I suppose. He didn't tell me."

Good old Mitch signaled to the waiter for his check. He gestured to the *Times* again. "According to this, you found Hilda."

"Yes."

"God," he said, "how awful." He took the check from the waiter and signed it. His credit rating was A1 in the hotel. "Did you know that I knew her, Mark? Washington. She was at Blue Haven down there for quite a spell—till just before she came up here. Marvelous performer. Nice, gay, happy girl, considering her problems."

"Problems?"

"She undoubtedly told you about her brother. Stanislaus Wolenski, victim of the upheavals in Poland. Probably in a labor camp somewhere, if he wasn't just shot and thrown in a ditch. Not unnaturally, she asked me for help." He shook his head. "People think we can find out anything in my shop, but even the CIA hasn't much chance of finding one man in that kind of turmoil. Needle-in-a-haystack department. He wasn't a big name in Solidarity. Could have got it in any number of riots involving Solidarity rebels and soldiers. You get me passed up to the roof?" He'd pushed back his chair and stood, pipe clenched between his teeth.

"I'll go with you," I said.

We walked across the lobby toward the roof car. "Police getting anywhere?" he asked. I told him I hadn't heard what progress they were making. "You know, Mark, I didn't sleep well last night. Didn't know about this, of course. But I was driving myself nutty trying to remember where I've seen that creep Hilda identified as being with Bob Ballard on the tenth floor—the one I pointed out to you in the Trapeze yesterday."

Do you know, I was looking at his hands. Good old Mitch had very big, very strong hands. Someone had had big hands that could reach right around Hilda's neck, Hardy had told us. Dick Berger, on the roof car, buzzed Chambrun and told him we wanted to come up. He got the green light.

We went silently up, up—and then out into the sunlight. Chambrun, Mrs. Haven, and Jericho were still sitting on the Man's terrace. It looked like a pleasant summer outing. Mrs. Haven in her garden hat, Jericho lounging over by the wall at the far end, looking down at the river, Chambrun sitting back in his wicker armchair, making a steeple out of his fingers as his hands rested against his chest.

"Thanks for coming, Prescott," Chambrun said.

"My pleasure," Mitch said. "They've really turned you upside down, haven't they, Pierre. How can I help?"

"Information you may have," Chambrun said.

"Anything I have—or can find out for you," Mitch said. "But so help me God, I simply can't place Ballard's killer. I know I've seen him somewhere, but it simply won't come."

"Of course it won't when you're trying," Mrs. Haven said. "You get to be my age and you try to remember names. You try and try, and then you give up. Then, suddenly, in the middle of the night, or when you're out shopping somewhere, you suddenly hear yourself shouting 'Guggenheim,' or whatever the name is. When you've stopped trying!"

"You're looking very lovely this morning, Victoria," Mitch said. "I'll try to stop trying and maybe, as you say, it will happen."

"Oh, it'll happen," Jericho said from his place at the wall. "Hey, look at this!"

Good old Mitch went over to him and glanced down over the wall. That wall is about four feet high, no way you can lose your balance.

"What is it?" Mitch asked.

"I just want you to see how far down it is to the street," Jericho said. "Forty-five floors! Quite a mess if you went over the side."

"I'm not fond of heights," Mitch said. He started to turn away.

Jericho made a lightning move. He grabbed Mitch's arm and twisted it behind his back in a painful hold. "You're going to have the pleasure of sampling the impact of the pavement when you land, Prescott," he said.

"What the hell is going on here!" Mitch almost shouted. He tried to free himself, but a further twist on his arm almost brought him to his knees. "For Christ's sake, Victoria, this man is crazy. Please—get help somewhere!"

"I don't think he's crazy," Mrs. Haven said, her eyes very bright, her voice very quiet. "You'd better tell him what he wants to know, or I may give him the old Roman gladiators' signal—thumbs-down!"

"What do you want to know, Jericho? For God's sake, ease up, man!"

Chambrun spoke, the hanging judge. "Where is Ruysdale?" he asked.

"Ruysdale? Are you talking about Betsy Ruysdale? I understood she'd taken a few days off. How would I know where she is? Jericho, for God's sake—!"

"Where is Ruysdale?" Jericho said. "It could be like drowning, you know, Prescott? Falling forty-five floors to the street—your whole life passes before your eyes—"

"Victoria! You can't just sit there and watch this maniac!" Mitch cried out.

"Where is Ruysdale?" Mrs. Haven asked.

"I don't know!" It was a cry of panic from good old Mitch. I guess he was beginning to believe.

"It's just come to me," Chambrun said in a deadly quiet voice, "like 'Guggenheim.' The lady provided you with her charms, her favors, in Washington because she wanted something from you. Help her find her missing brother. I suppose you said you'd do what you could, and didn't bother to do anything."

"At Mitchell's age it was enough for him to prove that he was still a man—with a young woman," Mrs. Haven said.

"I think you told her that you would help her if she would help you. There was a time coming when she could help—when she got here to New York."

"You're all crazy as loons!" Mitch protested.

"And the time came when she could help you. So elaborate! Larry Welch comes here. How much does he have on you, and whoever else is in it with you? The penthouse over there was safe for him, but it was also safe for you if I didn't provide Welch with extra protection. You and your people took Ruysdale, damn you!''

''Chambrun, you're out of your mind!''

''You took her, you warned me, and you were home free—you thought,'' Chambrun said. ''I don't know where the real Martin Stearns is, but you provided a fake. Fake passport, fake driver's license, fake ID— that's child's play for someone with CIA experience. Done every day, agents working under cover.''

''I told you he was a fake! If he was my man, why would I—?''

''Because you wanted to make yourself look good to us,'' Chambrun said. ''Your man had committed a murder, he was gone. Give him time—and you'd be, apparently, on our side.''

''But the man in the Trapeze, the man Hilda saw with Ballard?'' Mitch said. ''He was the murderer!''

''Not ever,'' Chambrun said. ''He was a plant of yours, just in case. You didn't expect to have to use him, but you had a piece of bad luck. Bob Ballard knew the real Martin Stearns from a job he'd held in Washington. When he was called up here to take 'Martin Stearns' down, he knew your man was a fraud. Your fake Stearns forced Ballard to stop this car at ten—a prearranged escape hatch, I imagine— took him out into the service area, and shot him. And that's where poor Hilda comes into the picture. You chose ten as an escape route because she had a room there. Now, if she will help you, you will find and free her brother for her. She is to come forward and say she saw Mr. X from the Trapeze with Ballard. The police have spent twenty-four hours looking for him. If they do find him, he'll have an alibi, won't he? You told Hilda this was secret CIA business, right? Then, last night, while you were wandering around from my office, you encountered her on the second floor. She invited you into Mark's apartment. There she told you she realized you were an accomplice in a murder. Do something about her brother or she'd blow the whistle on you. What did she do, start for the phone right there, when you threatened her?''

"This is madness!" Prescott said. "You can't prove any part of it."

"I don't have to," Chambrun said. "And it won't matter to you if you don't tell me where Ruysdale is. If you tell me, and she's safe, then it will be up to Lieutenant Hardy to prove out my theory. Maybe some fancy lawyer with Rhamadir's oil money behind him can get you off. But it isn't going to come to that unless I see Ruysdale alive and well. Where is she?''

Indecision is a pretty terrible thing to see on a man. Sweat was streaming down Mitch Prescott's face.

"Want to take another look down over the side, Prescott?" Jericho asked, and gave the man's arm a cruel twist.

"Wait, wait, wait!" Prescott cried out. He was sold, I guess. He turned to Chambrun. "You're into something so involved, Pierre, so complex, you can't begin to understand it."

"I don't want to understand it," Chambrun said. "Where is Ruysdale?"

Prescott's eyes narrowed, and I could almost hear the wheels turning behind them. Jericho made a sudden move. He spun Prescott around, grabbed him below the knees, and literally heaved him up on his stomach on to the parapet.

"*Wait!*" I swear Prescott's scream could have been heard in the United Nations Building, blocks away. Jericho took his arm again and pulled him down. Prescott's face had turned the color of ashes.

Chambrun got up from his chair. "We're running out of time, Prescott." He turned to Mrs. Haven. "If you'd like to go inside, my dear, there's no reason why you should witness this."

Mrs. Haven didn't move. "In a long life I've never watched a really bad man pay for his crimes," she said. "I think I'd like to stay."

That rather extraordinary statement from the lady made up Prescott's mind for him. Chambrun and Jericho weren't kidding.

"I think I won't choose to take a chance on whether this lunatic is serious or not," he said to Chambrun. "Take me to a telephone, and I'll do what I can to get Miss Ruysdale released."

"No chance," Chambrun said, a cutting edge to his voice. "You call, and you can instantly let them know something is wrong. They'll make new conditions and we're back to square one."

"What do you want, then?"

"An address, a location," Chambrun said.

"You try to break in on them, and there's no way the lady will get out alive," Prescott said.

"And if we don't, and you don't get in touch with them at prearranged times, how much chance will she have?" Jericho asked. "You see, Pal, there's one chance for her and one chance for you."

"I believe you're serious," Prescott said.

"Believe!" Jericho said.

Prescott moistened his lips. His mouth must have been dry as a sand box. "Believe it or not," he said, "she's just about a block away; old brownstone house. A block north and half a block east."

"Write it down," Chambrun said. "Here, Mark, take him this notebook."

"I hope he can write left-handed," Jericho said. "I don't want to find myself chasing him around the roof."

I took the notebook and my ball-point pen over to Prescott. He bent forward. The terrible pressure Jericho was exerting on his right arm, behind his back, must have been agonizing.

"I—I can't write this way," Prescott complained.

I handed him my ball-point and held the notebook against my chest. "Write," I said.

He scrawled awkwardly with his left hand. I was aware of the sour smell of fear on his breath. I took the notebook back to Chambrun, who glanced at it.

"Who lives in this house?" he asked Prescott.

"Retired couple own the building," Prescott said. "They occupy the basement and the first floor. They know nothing about what's going on. Ruysdale's being held on the second floor."

"How many people guarding her?"

Prescott hesitated. "It varies. Two to four or five. Pierre? . . ."

"Yes?"

"Isn't there some way we can handle this sensibly? I can get Miss Ruysdale free, you can forget your theories about me. It seems like a fair trade. Nobody will get hurt."

"I can't trust you to make a fair trade," Chambrun said. "You're already responsible for two murders. From what Welch tells us, there's no way to guess how badly you've sold out your own country. All you're thinking about at the moment is how to save yourself. You would betray me as casually as you'd puff on that bloody pipe of yours."

Prescott wiped at his face with the left sleeve of his jacket. "You don't have much time, Pierre," he said. "If I don't call them at twelve noon, on the dot, they'll know something has gone wrong."

Chambrun glanced at his wristwatch. "Fifty-three minutes," he said. "I'll remember that you gave me that much, Prescott," he said. He turned and was gone toward the roof-car canopy. Moments later we heard the car door open and close.

Jericho was still holding Prescott by the parapet. "Can I borrow your hat, Victoria?" he asked. "The sun is getting hot as hell out here."

Mrs. Haven took off her garden hat and handed it to me. I carried it across the terrace and gave it to Jericho. He put it on his head and gave me a grin. "How do I look?" he asked.

Mrs. Haven and I just sat there under the terrace awning, not talking, looking at Jericho in that grotesque hat, and his sweating prisoner. Time has a way of going slow and fast at the same time. Minutes seemed to drag past, and then I'd glance at my watch and they seemed to have been flying.

Fifteen minutes were gone and I heard the roof-car door open. I was on my feet, ready for anything. It was, unexpectedly, Chambrun. He came back and took over his wicker chair without speaking. Eleven-thirty—twenty minutes to twelve—two minutes to twelve. I saw Chambrun grip the arms of his chair so tightly his knuckles looked like white marbles. Somewhere in the distance we heard some sirens. It was twelve noon—on the dot!

Twelve-ten—twelve-fifteen—twelve-twenty—and then I heard the roof-car door open again. The first person I saw was Betsy Ruysdale! She came running toward us, aimed at no one but Chambrun. A business associate? Just an efficient secretary? she was in his arms—or should I say he was in her arms?

"It's all right, Pierre!" I heard her say softly. "It's all right, my dear!" She was comforting him as though it was he who had been in danger, not herself.

Then I saw that the roof car had been crowded. Jerry Dodd, Mike Maggio, and Lieutenant Hardy were coming toward us. Hardy walked over to where Jericho in his comic hat was holding Prescott.

"I'll take over here," he said. "Charges against you, Prescott, are murder, kidnapping, treason, and God knows what else that Chambrun and Larry Welch can make stand up for us. Let me read you this mumbo jumbo."

Prescott was read his rights.

Mike Maggio was grinning from ear to ear. "We did what you suggested, Mr. Chambrun," he said. "I went to the old couple who own the place, told them I was from the power company, there was a dangerous short circuit somewhere on the line. I was in. I went up to the second floor and knocked. Some guy answered from the inside. I told my story. He said he couldn't let me in just now. I argued. A second guy entered into the argument. We were yammering good and loud."

"Meanwhile I had gone up the fire escape," Jerry Dodd said. "Slipped in behind them and stuck my gun into one guy's neck. They gave up real easy! I let Mike in and we found Betsy in another room.''

"You could have phoned!" Chambrun said.

"Quicker to get here—only a block away," Jerry said. "Prescott told you there could be two to five guys. We didn't want to wait to phone and possibly have company."

Chambrun managed a smile. "Bless you, friends," he said. "And now—I have a hotel to run."

"What you need is rest, Pierre. I can handle things for you," Betsy Ruysdale said.

He gave her a smile I don't think I ever saw before. "I really believe you can, my love," he said. He glanced at me. "Tell our friend Welch we may have the last chapter for his story." He slipped his arm through Betsy Ruysdale's. "And tell him that now I'll protect him with an army if he asks for it." He led Betsy off into his penthouse. Hardy had already taken Prescott away.

"You know," Mrs. Haven said, "I don't quite understand why Pierre left it to you and Mike, Jerry. Why didn't he go with you?"

"We still don't know who is in this hotel working for Prescott's mob," Jerry Dodd said. "If Chambrun left the hotel, they'd have known something was cooking. Hard decision for the boss to make, but he made it. Turned out to be a piece of cake for Mike and me. We brought Betsy back, told Hardy what was up." Jerry laughed. "Well, there's a hotel to run," he said, and he and Mike took off." We'd hear it all, in full detail, over and over again later.

"Well, I for one could stand a good stiff drink," Mrs. Haven said. "You, Jericho? Mark? But first—one question to you, John Jericho. Would you have done it? Would you have heaved him over that wall?"

Jericho hesitated, smiling at her. "If I tell you I would, you may secretly loathe me for being a monster. If I tell you I wouldn't, you may hold me in contempt for being a coward. So I'll tell you the truth. I don't know. If the moment had come—I might have, I might not. Anyway, Victoria, it was your idea. 'I'd kill him,' you said."

"Ah well, I have to tell you, you're a marvelous actor," Victoria said. "You held me spellbound. The sad part of it all is, no portrait for me."

"My dear Victoria," Jericho said. "I'm going to paint a portrait of you that will be as famous as the Mona Lisa has been down through the centuries."

"And I," the old lady said, "am about to make martinis for all of us that you'll never forget. Shall we join Toto over at my place?"

Jericho took her arm. "Our pleasure," he said.

POISON PEN

A CHARLOTTE KENT MYSTERY

MARY KITTREDGE

Struggling each month to fill the pages of her new magazine for writers, Charlotte Kemp finds herself up the proverbial creek when she discovers her biggest, and very nearly only, contributor, Wesley Bell, sitting dead in her office swivel chair.

Then Charlotte discovers the hard way that she's at the top of somebody's must-kill list—an ending she'd like to skip entirely...if possible.

A DEB RALSTON MYSTERY

DEFICIT ENDING
LEE MARTIN

Ready or not, Ralston is back from maternity leave, haunted by the look of a young teller who is taken hostage and later killed— the first in a string of victims.

Deb Ralston is soon hot on the tail of the murderers and heading straight into deadly danger.

A Sheila Travis Mystery

MURDER
at
Markham

PATRICIA HOUCK SPRINKLE

First Time in Paperback

The body of beautiful bad girl Melanie Forbes is found wrapped in an Oriental rug in an unused basement storeroom of Chicago's elite school of diplomacy, the Markham Institute.

Sheila Travis, new administrative assistant to the president, has years of diplomatic experience behind her. Though unfamiliar with the protocol for dealing with a murder in one's new workplace, her nose for crime pulls Sheila—and her eccentric Aunt Mary—into the investigation.

"A delightful new sleuth makes her debut here."

—*Publishers Weekly*

First Time in Paperback

MIRIAM BORGENICHT

A tragedy turns into a living nightmare when health counselor Linda Stewart's adopted infant daughter is legally reclaimed by the baby's natural teenage mother— and both are found dead two days later.

Linda's agonizing grief is channeled into a burning determination to solve these senseless murders. While suspicions of drug involvement might explain the sudden fortune the young mother had acquired, Linda's subtle probing takes a seedy turn into black-market adoptions.

"Borgenicht's perceptive comments on troubling social issues generate plenty of tension." —Publishers Weekly

Mom
DOTH
MURDER
SLEEP

First Time in Paperback

James Yaffe

As chief investigator for the Mesa Grande, Colorado, public defender's office, Dave's reputation for solving the toughest cases had followed him all the way from New York City. So had his mother, his very unofficial homicide consultant. She did her best detective work over plates of pot roast and strudel, happily feeding her son while gleaning all the details of his latest case.

Now murder takes center stage at a local amateur theater production of *Macbeth*. Mom, of course, has some ideas of her own about whodunit as dark secrets, stormy passions, rage and jealousy unfold.

"Mom's detective style is the cream of a rich detective mystery."
—*The Drood Review of Mystery*

 WORLDWIDE LIBRARY
TM